HER GUARD

GARETH

JB TREPAGNIER

Her Guard Copyright © 2018 JB Trepagnier

All Rights Reserved. No part of this publication may be reproduced, stored in a retrieval system, or transmitted, in any form or in any means – by electronic, mechanical, photocopying, recording, or otherwise without prior written permission

Cover by Hannah Stern Jacob Designs

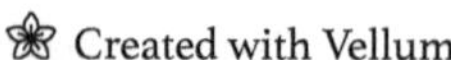 Created with Vellum

1

I thought Aiden just needed to get laid when he comes barging in the house from the salon about the little pinup girl he wanted to live with us. I got along with all my buddies, but after I got out the service, I had the most in common with Aiden. We were both angry. We'd hit up the bars on Bourbon Street and get shit faced. We'd find a pretty girl to bring home, use her for sex, then boot her out the bed the next morning.

Aiden and I were both angry drunks. Casey went straight into Academy when we got home and he'd somehow always heard about our bar fights and swoop in and drag us out of there before we got arrested. I was fine with this arrangement, but Aiden was miserable. Deep down, I knew that wasn't him. Aiden stopped going out, quit smoking, cut down on his drinking, and actually started trying to date girls instead of just using them for sex.

Andre and Casey were above drunken bar crawls and wouldn't go with me. Losing my drinking buddy eventually got me to straighten up a little too. Andre, Casey, and Aiden seemed happy to date around, so I tried it. I was miserable. Girls were confusing when you tried to talk to them. They liked joking Gareth who made them laugh, but if I tried to show them any of the things I was into, they weren't paying attention. They didn't want to sit through my favorite movies and they had horrible taste in music.

Andre, Casey, and Gareth could keep dating around hoping they found the one. I was done. If I needed to get my rocks off, I'd have a one-night stand, but even that started getting boring. I had decided I was totally done with women when Aiden barged in talking about the girl at the salon. Girls loved Aiden because he was this huge, sensitive man. I just knew that girl would get here and be totally gross around him. She'd disturb me when I was watching my movies or she'd ask me to turn my music down. No, we were fine the way we were.

I agreed to go to the salon to meet her with the others. I hoped they would all be on my side. I knew I was going to be outvoted when they all laid eyes on her. The girl was beautiful and she had this air of innocence about her, but I already knew that meant trouble. I was polite when I introduced myself and tried to joke with her. I knew I was in trouble when they all invited her to go out to eat with us.

That girl, at the time, I thought she must have been a witch. The longer I sat with her at the table, the more I wanted to see her smile again. She was knocking back those Bow Wows like she could be my new partner in crime for bar crawls. I found myself cracking up laughing when Casey tried to get her to slow down and she told him he must have a small dick to try to give her orders like that. I laughed even harder when she barfed all over the table and it splashed on Casey.

I thought maybe it wouldn't be totally horrible having her there. Maybe she'd actually be cool. And she was. She was hilarious and adorable. I decided to give her a little test. I asked her to watch one of my favorite movies. One that would be hard to sit through. It was a German horror film from the seventies and not a word of it was in English.

She shocked me. She sat back and watched the entire thing and even tried to critique it with me. She was smart and she had good taste in movies. I found myself falling for her and I knew damned well Aiden wanted her or he wouldn't have asked her to move in. I also found out Andre wanted to get to know her better too and Casey wouldn't have been working doubles if he wasn't avoiding his feelings like always.

We came to an agreement and I fought hard. I pulled out all my tricks to get her to pick me, but I was also honest. I'd never met anyone I wanted to be with before and I wanted Misty. I let her get to know the real me under all my jokes. I wasn't a jerk to her like I was most of the women I took up with. When Casey and I were fighting over Iris in high school, when he told me she picked him, I didn't realize at the time why it didn't bother me.

I just wasn't that into Iris. I knew it was going to bother me if she picked someone else. I'd break the arrangement we told her and try to steal her from them. I'd ruin friendships I'd had since kindergarten just to have her. We all ended up breaking our arrangement when she needed us the most. I took a punch to the gut from Aiden and threw Andre into a side table.

We had been beating up on each other and grunting like savages, completely unaware Misty had locked herself in her bedroom and it was upsetting her. It was Andre that suggested we all just share her. Casey was against it and Aiden took some convincing. I needed none. If that was the only way I could have her and keep my best friends, I would do it.

I didn't mean to blurt out her breaking our sex rule with all four of us. Sometimes, my mouth just said things before I could think about it to stop it from coming out. I was about to apologize and leave the room in mortification, but Misty shocked the hell out of me and was all for it. I knew she wasn't that experienced because she told me about her ex, but she was on fire that night. I don't think I'll ever forget that night we broke our sex rule together, even if there had been repeat performances and several nights alone with her.

But there was someone threatening my happiness and Misty. That, someone, had already trashed Aiden's shop and murdered his grandmother, who was really a grandmother to *all* of us. I was furious. Rook wasn't taking anything else from my little family.

I was going to go places Casey and Andre weren't willing to go. I trusted no one like Casey seemed to. He reported most everything to Leo and Bishop and Rook always found out. I'd never trusted Bishop anyway. Andre and I flat out told him we didn't want to be cops and he kept pressing. He even did it the night we came in with a traumatized Misty after Jake took her. He even tried to recruit *Misty* in front of us.

I looked into Bishop first, when Casey and Andre weren't around. I got into his work computer, but there was nothing there to lead me to his home computer. I didn't think there would be anything on his home computer either. Bishop had to be the most boring man on the planet. He never did anything he wasn't supposed to on his work computer. The man didn't even play solitaire when he got bored. He was constantly working, nonstop, like some drone.

I was pretty sure he got lunch breaks or fifteen-minute breaks like the rest of the planet, but he never took them. He seemed to always be looking at the files of Dillion, Serena, and now Grant. I cleared Bishop of being Rook pretty quickly. Mainly because he didn't seem to have a creative bone in his body and he bored me.

I cleared Leo too. Leo led me to his home computer because he was always making Skype calls with his wife to look at their children. Leo had to be some sort of saint. He didn't even look at porn on his home computer when he was home. Leo was all about his wife and kids.

I cleared both of them right away for being Rook. I didn't think they were knights or pawns either. So far, Rook's little chess pieces were sloppy on their computers. We always got their names, even if things went wrong when we tried to capture them.

If Bishop and Leo were the closest to Casey and they were the only ones who knew who was supposed to get arrested, where were the leaks coming from?

2

We were all in a sorry state after Granny was murdered and our one real lead to Rook died of poison only an hour before agreeing to give a statement. That was when we knew. We had to find a way to isolate pawns and knights and get to them away from the station. We had to get them to some sort of safehouse to see if they would give us Rook.

The problem was, Casey still wasn't cleared to go back to work. He was sleeping on the sectional with the rest of us, but he was moving around like he was in a lot of pain. We were all waking up one morning when Casey struggled to get up.

"Andre, call the men out for the bedroom. I can deal with the noise and the hammering. I just need a real bed and I think it would be good for us to have a bedroom instead of sleeping in the living room."

I totally agreed with him. We needed to be all sleeping together, but after several days on that sectional, my back was starting to hurt, even if that fucking thing cost seven thousand dollars and was made of memory foam. It still didn't beat a mattress. And sleeping in a bedroom Aiden designed holding Misty? That would be like paradise.

I ate breakfast with them like I always did. I'd sit and listen for Casey to drop any names he might be working with. If he mentioned a new name, I'd disappear to my bedroom to hack their work computer. He hadn't dropped any new names, so we were trying to figure out any connections between Serena and Grant and any other cops at the station. We'd been searching for that link since we got the news Grant had died.

Milo was an addition to our team none of us had expected. He'd been giving all of us private Skype lessons. We could ask him anything we wanted during our hour with him and he'd answer it as best he could. I was getting fond of this old man and wished Granny were still alive that we could tell her we liked him and she should stop seeing him in secret. Maybe the two of them could have married late in life and been happy.

Milo always checked in with us after breakfast. We reported anything we found and he did the same. He was always gruff and foul-mouthed when he addressed us and that was why I liked him. I was always on my best behavior when he was on camera.

"I found a connection," he said without saying hello. "Vera Granger was at ULL at the same time as Serena and Grant. She took the same online course with Rook and dropped out later that year. She's similar to your Jake and Dillion. She got excellent scores on her physical exam, but it took her a few times to pass the written. You know her, Casey?"

"Yeah. She's a real hard ass. She works in the evidence locker. She's more of a clerk than a cop. I would have thought she failed the written exam if she's just a clerk," Casey said.

"Yeah, well, when she did pass, it was by the skin of her teeth. Has she done anything to lose her badge?"

Andre got into it before I could. "Yeah, she did. She shot an unarmed teenager who was suspected of shoplifting. She's in evidence because she won't go to her therapy sessions to pass the psych eval to get her badge back."

"Or she's being told not to go to her therapy sessions because Rook needs her in the evidence locker. You say Jake was given drugs from evidence in LA? If he had an inside person in the locker, then all sorts of things could go missing," Milo said.

"Yeah, but right now, we have no proof except for the fact that she went to school with Serena and Grant," Casey said. "And I'm still not cleared to go back to work."

Milo shrugged. "That shouldn't fucking stop you. You've got two talented hackers at your disposal. Find the proof."

"Have your contacts found anything about Rook?" Misty asked. We had mostly been counting on Milo and the FBI to give us a little breadcrumb.

"Not a thing. Whatever Rook has been up to, he's never come to the attention of the FBI. They think I'm spinning them some New Orleans urban legend and the chess pieces on Aiden's shop and at Clara's house are some new gang. We all know that's a hot load of bullshit."

"Did you tell them about the texts Casey is getting?" Misty demanded. "What about the bomb Serena left that injured Casey? What the fuck about all that?"

Milo's eyes were sparkling. "I see why Clara ended up liking you. Gareth, I'm going to need you alone for our one on one."

I picked up my laptop and went back to my bedroom. "Casey, Andre, and Aiden all want to lock her in the house to protect her. We both know you're looking into things they aren't. *You* need to be the one to prepare Misty if she's taken. She's well protected, but it happened before."

"She was able to get us her location when Jake took her."

"That phone in the pocket trick isn't going to work a second time. I take it you know how to pick a pair of handcuffs?" I nodded. "You're going to be teaching Misty to fight and how to get out of any restraints they may put on her. Find a way to give her something, a pocket knife, anything, that she can get herself loose. That girl is special and I see why you're all in love with her. If it weren't for her, this evil man's plot would still be going unchecked. You understand me? You prepare that girl for any possible scenario if she's taken."

I nodded. I could do that. "I haven't found anything at the station. I've looked into everyone close to Casey at the station and they are all clean."

"On their computers, Gareth. We all know they are communicating by burner phones or something not tied to computers. Just because some of Rook's people have been careless doesn't mean he is. Rook's computer is probably spotless."

"Leo and Bishop are the only people Casey tells his plans to. I did get into Leo's home computer and I don't peg him for Rook or a knight or pawn. I don't think he would do anything to endanger his family. Bishop doesn't know about Rook, but he spends a lot of time looking at Dillion, Serena, and Grant's files like he's trying to figure this out too."

Milo winked at me. "I did some digging you boys can't. I have a full background report on both Leo and Bishop. I pegged them too. Leo has an exemplary record. He's former military like you boys. Graduated Academy with top marks, passed his exams with high scores, and he's earned several commendations since he earned his badge. Leo doesn't peg me as someone who would work for Rook and would report it if he was approached."

"And Bishop?"

"Bishop has a clean record too. He got to chief the hard way. There was no one granting him favors and he didn't have any miraculous busts that would have gotten him there faster. He made chief because he was a damned good cop and worked hard."

"So, we have nothing then. Fuck!" I yelled, punching my desk.

"Calm your tits, son. I didn't say that. All of you are concentrating so hard at looking at cops, but you haven't looked into who might be watching Leo and Bishop. You got into their computers pretty easily. Serena tried to get into Andre's. Does it not make sense Serena might have gotten into Leo and Bishop's computers too? She could be getting wind of things that way. Grant was different at first. You were able to arrest him. Think, Gareth. How was Grant different than Serena?"

"Casey told Leo through a cell phone conversation and told him not to tell anyone, not even Bishop. There wasn't really enough time for Leo to create any type of file on the computer, I don't think. He's got files on him now, but I don't think he did before."

"Well, there's your answer, asshole. You do what Rook and Serena are doing. You keep everything limited to cell phone conversations on a need to know basis and *nothing* goes on computers until you have everything you need. If someone wants to make a statement, you get them a lawyer *quietly* and don't tell anyone they're a squealer."

"Sorry, Milo. I feel like a total amateur when you tell us what we did wrong."

"You aren't a cop, Gareth. I don't think any cop would be prepared for Rook, not even Casey. He's apparently slid under the FBI's radar for decades and it took one of his knights fucking up with Misty to expose him. This is going to be a hard investigation for all of you and you need to prepare for the fact that he may get to Misty before you find him. Understand me? You prepare that girl for how to escape if he gets her."

"Yes, sir."

"I'm disconnecting and grabbing Andre. He needs to set up some sort of tracking on Leo and Bishop's computers so we can find who is accessing their case files. If he can trace it to Serena, then you'll probably find Rook with her."

I closed my laptop. I needed to make Misty some

sort of escape kit if she was caught, then teach her to use it. I had a random assortment of random junk that I kept because I thought it might come in handy one day. Most of it was just to prank Casey because it pissed him off so much, but I thought I had everything I needed in there.

I grinned. I was protecting my girl if Rook killed me to get to her and I couldn't later. She'd be able to get herself to safety, even if every single one of us died trying to prevent Rook from taking her.

3

I pretty much locked myself in my bedroom working on an escape kit for Misty. Rook would know by now she always kept her phone in her pocket. He would search her for phones and weapons. He wouldn't pay attention to a harmless bracelet and that was going to be how Misty got away from him.

I wove several leather strips together to fashion the bracelet, then I made it look like some sort of found object charm bracelet. Aiden liked to make art with found objects and I knew it was a big thing with do it yourselfers and crafts. Her bracelet looked like random objects, but I'd prepared for everything.

There were two safety pins and two bobby pins for picking handcuffs. I'd managed to hide an Exacto blade in a small, leather pouch. That could get her out if they used duct tape again and it could be a weapon. It could also be used on zip ties and if she could get to it, she could cut her way out of a straight jacket if they used that.

I'd thought of everything, but now I actually had to get Misty alone and teach her how to pick handcuffs and get herself out of other restraints. I didn't think it was a good idea to tell the others I was doing this. They didn't even want to think about Rook taking her. And Casey and Aiden really needed her right now. Especially Aiden.

I looked down at the bracelet I'd made. Milo said to think of everything and not rule anything out. I wanted to be like Milo. That was when it hit me. Dillion and Jake used duct tape. If Rook had someone do that again, she couldn't get to the bracelet. She needed a necklace. *And* if they decided to be savages and hog tie her, she wouldn't be able to get to the necklace. I needed to make an ankle bracelet for her too.

Satisfied I'd thought of everything, I stayed in my bedroom for the rest of the day making escape jewelry. I didn't even come out to eat. I found a protein bar that had to be ancient and ate it without tasting it. I didn't even hear Misty when she came in until she was right on top of me and was rubbing my back as I liked.

"Are you okay, Gareth? You've been locked in here for hours. I've been spending most of my time with Casey and Aiden. Is there something wrong?"

I turned around and pulled her into my lap. She always smelled unreal, like some really indulgent pastry Andre would make. She leaned into my chest and stroked my arms around her waist.

"Misty...," I started. I wasn't sure how she was going to take this jewelry and what I wanted to teach her. Would she get mad at me for doing all this?

"Out with it, Gareth. You can talk to me about anything."

"Milo and I have been talking. We need to be prepared for the real possibility that Rook might find a way to grab you. He wants me to prepare you so you can escape if that happens."

I felt her let out a breath, but I didn't know if it was an angry one or a sigh of relief. "Can you please, Gareth? If they break in here again and the choice is to leave with them or they kill all of you, I'll always leave with them. That was how Jake got me to leave. He threatened to shoot Andre."

"Misty, I know. And the only way that would happen would be if all of us were unconscious." I'd finished the bracelet, necklace, and anklet. I picked them up and showed them to her. "I made these. They have tools to get you out of any type of restraint once you've learned how. You have to wear them all the time. Promise me you'll never take them off."

"So, I have strip chess with Andre, naked yoga with Aiden, and picking handcuffs with you? Can we turn it into a game?"

I grinned. I could think of *several* things to do with her while she was tied up. I'd admit I was jealous of her chess games with Andre and I had no idea about naked yoga with Aiden. Made me wonder what she did with her alone time with Casey. Casey wasn't much for playing games and used to prefer being alone until Misty got here.

"I think I can find a way to turn this into a game." I had to ask. "What is your thing with Casey?"

"Casey and I just talk. That's what he needs the most. When do we start?"

"It's pretty late. We can start tomorrow. Will you stay tonight?" I knew I was asking a lot of her. She'd been running in all directions trying to pull Casey out his shell and Aiden was still dealing with his grief. I knew they needed her more than I did, but I'd always been a little selfish and I wanted Misty alone tonight.

"Have you been sitting in this chair hunched over jewelry all day?"

"Yeah. I just knew I needed to finish it now."

Misty stood up and grinned at me. "It sounds like what you need right now is a massage. Get naked and get on the bed."

She asked me to teach her what I'd learned at massage school. I really wasn't there long before I dropped out, but I'd learned the basics. Being around half-naked women in sheets was just too hard and I had no idea why I ever thought that was a good idea. I wasn't all that happy being a security guard either, but I was good at it and my client paid me a shit ton of money just to sit at home unless he needed me.

I had stripped out my clothes in seconds and took a running leap at the bed. Misty giggled. I rolled onto my back when I heard the rustling of her removing her clothes. I'd been with plenty of attractive women I'd picked up at bars, then discarded the next morning, but Misty topped them in all ways.

Not only was she amazingly cool to just hang out with, she was drop dead gorgeous and had a banging body. And tonight, she was mine. She tackled me on the bed and I gladly let her. I loved it when she got goofy and playful, especially with all this Rook shit going on.

"On your stomach, Gareth!" she ordered.

"Um, Misty, when you tackle me naked, I kind of have a raging boner right now."

She just shrugged. "You make me wait all the time. You look tense, Gareth. I'll get to your boner later."

It took some adjusting, but I was able to lie on my stomach comfortably, even if my dick was aching for her. I'd never been with a woman who wanted to pamper me before and found that I liked it when Misty did it our first day alone together. No one had rubbed my back like that before. It was always drunken sex and I was always over it the next morning.

Misty straddled my waist and I felt her fingers petting my back like she had that first day. I shivered. I had no idea I would like it that much until she did it. It made my whole body tingle and a warm feeling in my stomach. It made me feel loved that someone cared enough to do something simple like rub my back just because it made me feel good.

Her petting moved to a massage and I realized how tense my back had been from sitting hunched over at my desk all day. Misty always said I had magic hands, but she had to be much better at massage than I ever was. I felt like a was floating in a scented pool of warm water and I was fighting falling asleep.

My eyes flew open when I felt her nip the tip of my ear. "Don't you dare fall asleep on me. I haven't been alone with you in what seems like forever and I need a little of Gareth's special brand of love."

"And how do you need it tonight?"

"I said I would give your boner attention when I was done with your back. Why don't you roll over?"

She didn't have to ask me twice. I knew her ex never went down on her and I had no idea if she could do the things she could with her mouth because he demanded she do what he wouldn't. That guy was a total idiot, but if he hadn't been, Misty would be living with him in New York instead of in my bedroom right now about to suck my dick.

I don't know why her ex popped in my head right that minute. I always got angry when I thought about him and how he treated her. He must have been a complete shit stain to not realize what was right in front of him and not cherish it. I didn't want to be anything like her ex. I didn't want her going down on me because she thought she had to. I'd love the hell out of it and return the favor, of course, but right that minute I was getting angry thinking about all the head she might have given getting nothing back.

"Let's do this another way," I said, sitting up. "I want to taste you while you're giving me attention. I want you to sit on my face while you do it. I want you to feel good too."

Misty caressed my cheek. "That's what I love about you, Gareth. You always worry about what I'm feeling."

She seemed to like it when Casey did it, so I swatted her ass. "On my face, wench!"

She giggled and did what I asked. I wrapped my arms around her thighs and pulled that delicious pussy to my mouth. I lapped at her honey, fucking her with my tongue. I groaned when I felt my dick slide deep down her throat. That girl had some sort of unreal gag reflex. I tongued her little nub with slow circles and she groaned on my dick.

She started grinding against my tongue, so I loosened my arms around her thighs so she could fuck my face. She was wild that night and I was totally into it. She was grinding her pussy into my face while working my cock with her mouth and hand. I was trying to hold off and just enjoy the ride. I didn't want to blow my load right then because she was all mine tonight and I intended to have her until I couldn't anymore.

I tried to concentration on flicking my tongue on her clit while she furiously rode my face instead of the buildup in my balls. Luckily, Misty didn't last much longer. She had this little cry she made when she came that was music to my ears. It was muffled by my dick this time, but I could spend the rest of my life making her make that noise. She collapsed on my chest panting.

"I'm sorry, Gareth, I need a minute."

That was also music to my ears. I'd made her come so hard, she needed to recover from it.

"Snuggle with me, Misty."

"But—"

"I can wait while you recover."

With Misty, it had never been about my needs. Well, except for the night I was so eager to break our no sex rule with her, I just blurted out we all do it together right then and there. My thought process when she asked was that we'd just start fighting again and run her off. If I had been thinking clearly, I wouldn't have said something that may have run her off again. I think Misty even shocked herself when she agreed to it unless that little minx had been thinking about it this whole time. I needed to apologize to her.

"Misty, that night I suggested we break our no sex rule together, did you just agree to it because you thought that was what we wanted? We never talked about that, it just kind of came out my mouth. Did I put pressure on you?"

Misty laughed and rubbed her face into my chest. "I'll admit to having thought about it before I went to bed before I started spending the night alone with one of you. I wasn't offended when you asked and I didn't have to think that hard about it before I agreed. That night was special for me. Are *you* regretting it, Gareth?"

"That night *was* special to me too, but I needed you to know, we didn't talk about that. I just blurted it out and instantly regretted it. I needed to know you haven't been doing all this because you thought it was something we discussed and wanted of you."

"Gareth, please. I think it would be any girl's fantasy to have what I have here. Four hot guys I'm in love with and they love me back? They'll do anything for me. I love all of you together and treasure it when we're alone too."

And I treasured my time with her too. I rolled her onto her back and stroked her cheeks. "I want to make *all* your fantasies come true, Misty. Tell me one and we'll make it happen tonight."

Her cheeks flushed pink and it was adorable. "I have had one since you told me you were a massage school dropout. Do you still have your oils and a blanket you don't mind getting stained?"

I was out of bed in seconds. I didn't have any of my

oils from massage school, but since I knew Misty liked my backrubs, I had bought several scented oils to rub her back. I had black silk sheets on my bed and I would gladly ruin them to make her fantasy come true. My goal in life now was to protect Misty and worship her as much as I could.

I went to a drawer and started pulling bottles out. "I've got vanilla, sandalwood, rose, honeysuckle. Which one do you want?" I still had no idea what she had planned with the oils, but I was going to bring her fantasy to life tonight.

"Vanilla. And I don't want to ruin your sheets. Do you have like, a tarp or huge blanket we could put over the bed?"

I cocked an eyebrow at her. What was my kinky little goddess planning for tonight? I had tarp left over because I liked to change the color of my walls often. I pulled one out my closet and draped it across the bed. I handed the bottle to Misty and just waited for her to command me.

She squirted the bottle on her perky breasts, then grabbed my hands. "Rub it everywhere, Gareth. Oil up my entire body."

She didn't have to ask me twice. I spread the oil all over her torso, massaging it in. Her oil slick breasts felt amazing in my hands. I worked the oil over her entire body. I massaged it into her toned thighs and she turned around so I could work it into her back and perfect ass. Her entire body was glistening with oil, the dimmed light glistening on her perfect body. My dick was aching for her after how good it felt oiling her up, but I awaited her command. This was her fantasy.

I had no idea what she was doing when she started reading the back of the bottle. She looked up and gave me a kittenish grin. "Did you know this was edible when you bought it? It's your turn now."

I gulped. If she intended to give me the same treatment I gave her with the oil and she touched my dick at all, I'd probably blow my load all over the bed and ruin this fantasy before it was completed. She must have seen the look on my face.

"Relax and enjoy it, Gareth. Lie down."

This was much more sensual than her back massage earlier. As she rubbed the oil into my body, she was also rubbing her slick body against me. She hadn't even gotten to my lower body yet, but I was about to explode from her oiled breasts rubbing against my chest. I was liking this fantasy. Hell, if I'd had a lick of sense while I was in massage school, *I* would have come up with this fantasy.

She completely avoided my dick when she was rubbing oil into my thighs. Maybe she knew it would go off or she had other plans. This was her fantasy, so I was going to lie here and let her do whatever she fucking wanted to me. I rolled over on my back when she asked. I wasn't quite sure about it when she started massaging oil into my ass and her fingers kept slipping. I'd kicked a girl I took home from the bar without even fucking her after she wanted to stick her pinky up my ass.

I decided to just let Misty go for it if that was what she wanted. I'd asked for her ass and she didn't even hesitate when she gave it to me. I braced myself when she parted my ass cheeks, but I felt her tongue there instead of her finger. I was about to slam on her on the bed and fuck her brains out. I had no idea it felt that good. I groaned and tried to control myself.

"Do you like this, Gareth? I like it being done to me, but I've never done it to a man before. You said we could do my fantasies tonight. Do you want me to stop?"

"God, Misty, if you keep doing that, I'm going to pin you down and have my wicked way with you before you can finish your fantasy."

Misty just giggled and went back to tonguing my ass. I was grinding my dick into the bed wishing it was her. It didn't seem like she was ever going to let up. I could feel the pressure building up in every area of my body and I thought I was going to erupt before she spanked my ass and told me to roll over. I even liked her spanking me and I knew that was a thing Casey like to do to her.

Her entire body was glistening from the oil in the dimmed light of my room. Her gray eyes were hooded with desire as I watched them roam over my body. I nearly blew my load when she slid down on my dick. There was nothing I liked more than watching her when she was bouncing on my dick, but it was an entirely new sensation when she pressed her oiled chest onto mine and started riding me that way.

Both our bodies were slick with the oil. Her hard nipples were sliding all over my chest. Her face was buried in my neck and all I could smell was the irresistible smell of that shampoo she used and the vanilla in the oil we used. The two played off each other and I just wanted to eat Misty. She had herself wrapped around me like a koala bear and I was clutching her waist trying to pull her as close to me as possible. I'd never felt this close to a woman before.

Misty sped up and we were both having issues controlling ourselves. I was trying to wait for her as she bounced on my dick and rubbed her hard nipples all over me. She bit down on my neck when she came. The pinch of her teeth and the feel of her pussy fluttering around my dick set me off. I grabbed her waist even harder and thrust into her hard as my body was wracked with one of the most intense orgasms of my entire life.

I collapsed on the bed when my body was spent. Misty was nuzzling my neck and giving me little nips and kisses. "Holy shit, Misty. I love your fantasies."

"I've wanted to do this with you since that first day you rubbed my back. It was how I wanted to break our no sex rule. I never thought it would happen because I didn't want to pick."

My chest seized up. I thought that was just a Misty fantasy she did because I asked her to. I had no idea it was a fantasy she had *about me.* It felt good to know she thought about this that first day in my room and I was able to make it come true for her. I vowed to make all of her fantasies come true if she chose to share them with me.

"Gareth?" she asked, kissing her way up to my mouth. "I'm all oiled up and slick *everywhere.* It would be a shame for you not to fuck my ass tonight when it's all ready for you."

I gulped. She was the first woman I'd had sex with that way. I asked after seeing her do it with Casey and that she seemed to like it. She must *really* like it if she was asking for it now, Tonight, I had Misty alone and I told her I would make her fantasies come true. If she wanted that, I was going to fuck her ass while fingering her clit until she couldn't stand it anymore.

I didn't think it was possible after the orgasm I'd just had, but just thinking about it had my dick at attention again. Misty grinned when she felt me stiffen inside her.

I had a feeling my love was going to keep me up all night. I just hoped I had enough stamina to keep up with her.

4

I must have gotten the most peaceful night sleep since Misty told us Jake was after her, then we found out about Rook. It's easy to sleep and forget when you're up most of the night involved in your woman's fantasies. I slept snuggled with Misty smelling her sweet perfume and vanilla. I didn't even worry about what was going to be waiting for me when I woke up. My thoughts were only consumed with the woman in my arms as I drifted off to sleep.

I expected Misty to be gone when I finally woke up. I just expected her to join the others and deal with the Rook situation. Or she would go be with Aiden and Casey since they needed her more than I did. I was surprised when my eyes fluttered open that she had her head propped up on her hand watching me sleep and she was playing with my hair. She was still nude, but I noticed she had gotten up in the middle of the night and put the jewelry I made for her on.

"Never take this off until Rook is caught, Misty," I said, fingering the necklace.

"Oh, Gareth," she chuckled. "I'm going to keep wearing them after Rook because you made them for me. I know what they are meant for, but they are pretty in their own way."

I was about to kiss her when my computer started ringing I had a call. It had to be Milo. He was the only one I ever spoke to over video chat. I threw some shorts on and told Misty to get dressed. By the time I answered, Milo apparently already knew she was with me and just sat there tapping his finger on the desk impatiently until she got dress and came to sit in my lap.

"You got any fight training, girl?"

"I studied ballet for fifteen years and I taught yoga back in California. I've never thrown a punch before, but I'm not totally helpless. I try to keep my body in ballet shape. It might not look like it, but I have good upper body strength."

"And I don't want you using it at all. Your fists are useless if they've got guns and bombs. I intend for *all* of you to come through this alive, then I want to see the people who hurt my Clara strung up by their thumbs. I think all of us would like five minutes alone with them in their cells, but that Bishop is too fucking boring or too worried about protocol to have faces smashed in on his watch, even if they deserve it."

"I really thought Bishop was Rook or would lead us to him. It just makes sense," I ranted, running my fingers through my hair. "He seems like he's trying to find the connection too, even if Casey hasn't told him about Rook."

"Bishop could still be the source of the leaks. Andre installed a logger on his work computer so we can see if anyone is accessing it. You should go talk to Andre and see if he's got any hits. Misty, is that necklace what I think it is?" Milo asked.

"Gareth made me a necklace, bracelet, and anklet. He's going to start teaching me how to get out of restraints next."

"Good thinking, Gareth. Cover all your bases. I also want you to get Misty mace and a taser. They make them to go on keychains now because men can still be savages and hurt women. I'm sending you a link through chat. Order it and go see Andre."

Milo disconnected. The link took me to a webpage that had the mace and the taser together. You could even get the taser in different colors. I had no idea if that mattered to Misty. I didn't think it would, but I asked.

"Just get me one that works. I don't want to put glitter on a pink taser just because it's on my keychain. I just want one to drop Rook or Serena if they come near me."

"That's my girl," I said, hitting purchase. I didn't expect her to care what color it was, but I was about to pick for her like I was telling her what to do. The page defaulted to black and she said she didn't want to pick, she wanted functional, so I went with that.

Misty and I walked into the living room holding hands. Everyone was in their usual positions on the sectional, but Casey was pacing as best he could with his injury and seemed pissed about something. I had my laptop under my arm and set it up next to Andre.

"What's got Casey pissed?"

"I keep telling him it won't stop us, but he thinks it's an obstacle. I put loggers on Bishop and Leo's computer and I've gotten hits. Rook's knights and pawns have gotten a little smarter or Serena finally wised up and started using a VPN to hide their IP. Want to hack a VPN service, Gareth?"

"I already have. Remember when I got that senator busted for child porn? He thought he was safe using a VPN. Didn't slow me down."

"You see, Casey?" Andre called to Casey's back. "Gareth and I have both done this before."

Aiden was also in a bad mood. Rightly so. His mood hadn't improved much since Granny, even if Milo was talking to him every day and Misty was trying to help him.

"Even if you do find who is behind the VPN, it's just going to be another knight or pawn and Rook will get to them before they talk if they decide they want to."

"What is Milo telling you anyway?" Casey said, whirling around. Milo was teaching all of us to look at things in different ways so we *could* get Rook. Milo wanted blood for Granny just as much as the rest of us did.

"Milo and I talk about Granny. We share memories," Aiden grumped.

"Milo talks to the rest of us about strategy. We have a plan if we get a new name," Casey said. "Rook won't know about it."

"He always seems to know, Casey. He knew killing Granny would hurt all of us!"

"But he *didn't* know she was dating ex-FBI," I

pointed out. "Rook has no idea if Milo can convince them he's real, he'll have the FBI after him too."

"Aiden, everyone eventually messes up," Misty said, playing with Aiden's long hair. "Rook or Serena will get careless and everything now is being done off computer where they can't find anything. If it's Serena using the VPN, Gareth or Andre will get a location. If we find Serena, we find Rook."

"I don't think Rook is going to risk losing his Queen and exposing himself. Whoever is using the VPN is going to be a knight or pawn, but they might give us Rook," Andre said. "I just need to figure out what VPN this IP address is using."

"If it's not a stable VPN, the connection may drop while they are in Leo or Bishop's computer and we'll get a *real* IP," I said.

Andre had just given me access to his spyware, so I started watching the logs. It was pretty slow going since we had nothing right now. Our last mark was poisoned in his jail cell and we didn't have another one yet. I was getting bored watching my computer. I was watching Leo and Andre was watching Bishop. I didn't actually get any hits on Leo's computer until Leo would have taken his lunch break.

Leo always left the office for lunch and went home to eat with his wife. I didn't know Leo at all aside from what Casey told me, but I wanted to have the kind of relationship he had with his wife with Misty. He always ate lunch with her and he couldn't get through his day without video chatting with her at least twice. Leo was much older than us and his kids were almost teenagers now, but he was still totally smitten with his wife.

I saw the IP address pop up on the logger and decided to remote into Leo's computer too so I could see what they were up to. Whoever it was opened a file search and did a scan for new files. They looked at Leo's new cases. I opened a new window and pinged their IP. They were definitely using a VPN. It showed some generic server in Canada. I had no idea if they were using Canada because the VPN service didn't have a tunnel in the United States or they thought they were smart and we'd actually think they were really in Canada.

I still had the VPN program I wrote when I saw that senator at a party with my boss feeling up a fifteen-year-old. I fired it up and let it do its thing.

I grinned at Andre. "We're looking at the Nimbus VPN. Now that we know, I just need to let a few programs run in the background and we'll have their real IP. No hacking a VPN required."

"Good show, man," Andre said, clapping me on the back.

I knew Andre was right. My program was just going to lead us to a knight or a pawn. Rook wasn't going to put his queen back on the board, especially now that I knew they were lovers. We'd get another knight or pawn, but if we played our board right, it would give us Rook.

5

I thought I'd be sleeping alone again that night. Casey and Aiden needed Misty and they were mostly sleeping in Casey's huge bed and doing god knows what. I was surprised when Misty suggested us all sleeping on the sectional again. I wanted to think it was her night with me and she just wanted to be with me too, but she was probably thinking about Andre too.

The problem was that there was only one of Misty and four of us that were desperately in love with her. Andre was paying extra to get that bedroom built for all of us and Casey wasn't the only one who got really annoyed by all the hammering and construction noises, but I wasn't as vocal about it as he was. He hadn't said a word since he asked for them to come back, but he had this vein that would twitch in his forehead every time that brooding thing he was famous for was brimming under the surface.

We all started pushing the sectional together. I thought we were going to all just sleep. We hadn't all played together since Granny was murdered. Aiden was still walking around in a haze and a foul mood. I was pretty sure Aiden wouldn't be up for anything except sleeping and eating. I was flat out shocked when Aiden asked Misty if she would dance for us again. I knew what that meant.

Misty had done a slow, sultry strip tease for us before. The music she put on this time was totally different. Misty was doing this sort of rage striptease. She was practically ripping her clothes off in this furious dance she was doing. She danced over to Aiden and pulled him over to the center of the room.

Aiden had never been aggressive. He'd been picked on when we were younger until he hit his growth spurt and towered over everyone in our class. Misty was dancing around him and roughly ripping his clothes off too. I could see Aiden start coming back to us as she ripped his clothes off, but damned if I didn't want to be where he was having my goddess naked dancing around me and stripping my clothes off like that.

I was stroking my cock through my pants watching Misty's little show. Aiden actually *growled* and picked her up to carry her over to the sectional. I was wondering if the rest of us were invited when Aiden slid Misty down his dick. I knew Aiden needed this, so if he just expected us to watch, I'd go jerk off in my bedroom and come back to the sectional.

"All of you get naked and get over here to please our woman," Aiden gruffed.

He didn't need to ask any of us twice. I could tell Casey was still hurting. He got naked first and sat next to her so she could grab his cock with her tiny hand.

Andre and I just stared at each other wondering what to do next. Aiden was practically devouring Misty's next.

"I want Andre in my mouth," Misty gasped. "He tastes like honey."

Andre wasn't about to argue with that, but I didn't know if I had permission to take her ass again. She'd given me permission once, but I wasn't about to go there and do that to her without either asking or her asking me. Before she took Andre in her mouth, she looked me right in the eye.

"What are you waiting for, Gareth?"

I'd never taken Misty like this before. Not with one of my friends already buried in her pussy. Casey and Andre had. I hadn't because she never asked me to before. I wanted to feel that more than anything, but I never knew if that was something she was wanting that night. I never wanted to ask because I knew she'd probably say yes even if it wasn't something she was into right then.

I never knew how much of what we got up to when we were all together was all her idea or ours. That was part of why I asked her to tell me a fantasy and I would make it come true. I'd never cared what a woman I was taking up with wanted before, but I cared with Misty. I never wanted her to do anything just because she thought I wanted to.

"Gareth?" Misty said.

"Sorry, Misty. Are you sure this is what you want?"

Misty chuckled. She arched her back and started grinding on Aiden's cock. She threw her head back. "Oh, yes, Gareth. I come quite hard this way."

My dick was twitching watching her slowly ride

Aiden. I was out of my clothes in seconds. Misty came just while I was fingering her ass and kissing her neck and I was turned on as hell watching her suck off Andre and ride Aiden. It was like heaven when I slid into Misty. Her ass was tight as hell and I could feel Aiden inside her.

This was unreal. Misty's cries were muffled by Andre's cock, but she was practically screaming. Apparently, my little minx really did love this. She wasn't faking either. She came again and collapsed across Aiden's chest. Aiden wrapped his arms around her waist and we both continued to pump her with our cocks. Aiden came first and I soon followed. I pulled out of her and collapsed on the sectional.

Casey and Andre weren't done yet. "Get over here, little Misty," Casey growled.

"I want to try something," Misty said. We all perked up when Misty said she wanted to try something.

I found myself getting hard again when I watched her face away from Casey and slide her ass down his cock. That little minx was practically in a straddle split with her legs open. She started fingering her clit.

"Get over here, Andre," she purred.

He practically leapt over the sectional and buried his cock in her pussy. I watched Casey and Andre take her like Aiden and I had taken her, with just a little twist. Andre moved her hand and was working her clit. I was pumping my cock with my hand while I watching Andre and Casey fuck Misty. Misty was howling before the two of them were finished with her.

We all piled onto the sectional to sleep. Misty had

her head on Aiden's chest and I was snuggled up behind her spooning her.

"Guys?" Misty said. "I can't tell you how much this arrangement means to me. I'm glad you came into my bedroom that night and stopped me from running. I'm happy there's no drama or fighting and we have what we have. I love my time alone with all of you, but what we just did? My entire body is shaking. I love all of you. Together or separate, I love you all. Promise me it will always be like this."

I kissed the back of her head and swore. I would always try to make her happy, even if it meant sharing her. There were only two things that stood in the way of our happiness and I'd take care of that when we woke up. I needed to find Rook and Serena and I needed to prepare Misty if they did get to her.

6

—————

Even if I slept right next to Misty on the sectional, I felt hollow if I woke up and she was out of my arms. I wandered into the kitchen and she and Andre were cooking together. That was a first. Misty was the only person in the house Andre would allow to use his kitchen, but he never shared it with her at the same time. Misty was adorable when she cooked. She danced around the kitchen singing and shaking her ass.

I tried to remind myself Misty and I had our own thing as I jealously watched Misty dancing around Andre and swatting at his ass with a pot holder. When she would get him, he would turn from the skillet and passionately kiss her. It made me feel bad because I knew once she learned to escape, I wouldn't have my own thing with her anymore. Andre had *more* than one thing. They did strip chess and now cooking together.

I left the room while they cooked to check my program. I was sure my face was betraying me and after what Misty said last night and what I promised, I didn't want her to see me getting jealous. Apparently, I wasn't the only one who had that idea. Casey and Aiden were already out there in foul moods. They all woke up before I did and couldn't deal with the scene in the kitchen either.

Casey was doing his broody thing and looked like he was trying to stop himself from storming off to his bedroom and punching things, which is what he used to do before Misty got here. Aiden was just staring off into space scratching King's belly. I just shrugged. We were all dealing with the same thing and if we spoke it out loud, we'd probably start screaming and hurt Misty.

I opened my laptop and ran my program. I'd apparently slept in as it was almost eleven. I grinned to myself as I realized someone had accessed Leo's computer when he must have been out of the office. My program already had a real IP and installed malware while this chess piece was on Leo's computer. I was hoping I'd get Serena, but I already knew Rook probably took her off the board.

I didn't have time to get into their computer because Andre and Misty called us in to eat. I decided to just break the foul moods of Aiden and Casey by bringing up I had a hit. It cheered me up and I didn't want their sour faces making Misty unhappy when she'd just been singing and dancing around the kitchen. As I expected, Casey perked up and Aiden just stayed grumpy. I don't think Aiden's mood was ever going to get better until we had the man who put the hit on Granny.

Breakfast was excellent like always. There were perks to living with the son of a five-star chef, even if that son was really weird about not telling anyone to touch his kitchen. He wouldn't even let us go in there to make ourselves a fucking sandwich. If we were hungry, we had to tell him and he would cook something. I knew it was Andre's little way of taking care of us, but he could be a bit of a control freak sometimes.

We all inhaled our food since I might have something that would bring us closer to Rook. Casey was still moaning about not being cleared for work yet. Casey never complained about pain. The man got caught in a bomb blast and the only thing he bitched about was not being able to work.

When we went back into the living room, I sent Andre what I had. The idea was that I would hack the IP I had and Andre would hack the person's other computer, whether it be work or home. Casey was back to pacing and wondering which coworker betrayed him this time. When I looked over at Andre, he had a Skype chat going with Milo. Milo! He needed this too.

I opened Skype and sent Milo everything I had. That ornery old man was a damned good hacker in his own right. He sent me a message back to quit dicking around and get everyone a name. That was kind of exactly what I expected from him.

As I expected, it wasn't Serena and this little pawn was more careful than Rook's other hackers. They were using a VPN and not doing stupid shit like trying to hack Andre from their work computers. This pawn was using their home computer and must have thought that VPN kept them safe. It was still stupid and careless for someone like Rook.

"Peter Jordan ring a bell?" I asked. "He's doing this from home and not work."

"Pete?" Casey asked, his jaw hanging open. "Pete works in homicide. I'd never take him for one of Rook's."

Andre was glued to his keyboard. "Well, let's see why Pete has been home so much instead of working in homicide."

"I can tell you that without digging into his computer," Casey said. "He's recovering from back surgery. Pinched nerve. He's been on temporary disability since right before everything with Jake. Pete is really old-fashioned. I didn't take him for knowing how to hack."

"Yeah, well, none of us took Milo for ex FBI, a hacker, or fucking my granny when he showed up at her funeral," Aiden grumped.

Misty started playing with Aiden's long hair. "If we can get Pete to talk, maybe Milo's FBI friends will take notice and finally get involved."

"It's too easy. One of Rook's pawns just *happens* to be injured at home where Leo can grab him without the attention of the station? Serena will probably have another bomb waiting."

I laughed maniacally as I ripped through Pete's computer. "We don't have to grab Pete at home. He's got a Mac syncing with an iPhone and I've got access to his calendars. The man practically plans when he takes a shit. There's plenty of opportunities to grab him when he's not at home. Doctor's appointments, grocery shopping, he even has it scheduled when he sits down to check Leo's computer."

A Skype call came in from Milo, so I answered.

"Are you seeing this horse shit?" Milo asked. "He left an evidence trail on the cloud. I made a phone call and I have an office you can question him in that Rook won't know about. It's FBI property and I had to do a *lot* of ass kissing to get permission to use this office. I had to promise some sort of proof that this Rook I've been blabbing about is actually real, so don't fuck this shit up or you'll ruin my reputation and we won't have my boys on our side to take down the turd that killed my Clara."

Casey's mood had instantly lifted and he was back in cop mode. "I understand and everything you taught me will go to use. I'll arrange everything with Leo. Phone conversations only. No texts, no voicemails, no emails. Nothing happens unless we are speaking. No trail this time. I think it would be best to have Leo approach Pete at the grocery store. He's less likely to make a scene there."

"Casey, get your ass in gear and get Leo on the phone. Gareth, I believe I gave you and Misty an assignment?" Milo said, tapping his finger on the table. He always did that, the finger tapping like he didn't like to sit still.

No one knew what my assignment was with Misty and no one asked. No one questioned the odd jewelry she was wearing either. She said she wanted to turn what we were doing into a game, but I had no idea what my gray-eyed little minx had planned.

I was about to find out.

7

I decided to teach Misty to pick handcuffs first since it was the hardest. She sat in an overstuffed chair in my bedroom while I dug out my hand-cuffs. Misty cocked an eyebrow at me.

"Do I want to know why you have handcuffs, Gareth? Casey, I understand. If you used them on other women, I don't think I want to know."

I kissed the tip of her nose. "These are for work in case I need to restrain someone who tried to hurt my client. I've never used them on another woman. Almost everything I've done with you, I've never done with another woman before. I was in a bad head space for years until you got here."

"Oh, Gareth, why didn't you say something?"

"I'd like to just forget about it. I'm not like Casey where I have to stew on it endlessly or talk it out like Aiden. When I'm done with something, I'm just done."

"And me and this arrangement? When you're done with it, are you just going to stop talking to me or move out?" She looked hurt, like I had already done this. "I see how you all look at each other sometimes. Like you aren't totally okay with what we are doing."

I pulled her out the chair and sat back down with her in my lap. The handcuffs could wait. "It's just all new for us and we are getting used to it. It's hard for us to not get jealous sometimes, but we are all working on it. There's four of us and one of you. You can't be in four places at once and we understand that. I think all of us love you so much, we don't want to do anything to fuck this up.

"I don't think I'll ever be done with you or this situation. I've never loved anyone like I love you. If loving you means having you love Andre, Aiden, and Casey, I can handle that. And to be honest, I think we all thought we'd hate it, but last night on the sectional with you was hot as fuck."

She giggled and nuzzled my neck. "Why did you hesitate last night?"

"Honestly? I didn't know if doing that hurt you and you were just doing it to please us."

"God, no Gareth, it feels amazing when all of you are doing that to me. I have multiple orgasms and they are so intense, I'm shaking for hours after. I certainly didn't have this much sex before I got here and I had no idea it could be this good. That first day in your bedroom alone was enough to show me what I'd been missing."

"Be careful, Misty. I'll have to remind you instead of teaching you how to pick these cuffs."

She gave me a sly look. "You promised me we could turn it into a game."

My dick got hard and the chance I was actually going to teach her to pick cuffs today was getting smaller. "And what kind of game did you want to play?"

"I liked acting out my fantasy with you. I have plenty more that concern just you. If I succeed, you let me act out a fantasy with no question."

"Shit, Misty, I would have done that anyway."

"I know, but now we have a game we can play and I love games. Not the one Rook is playing, of course, but the games I have with the four of you. Now, teach me how to pick handcuffs while Casey moves in on one of Rook's men."

I closed the handcuffs on Misty's wrist. I knew I needed to be teaching her, but damned if my mind wasn't on all the things I could do to her with those handcuffs on. Then, it went to what sort of fantasy she would bring out when she got out of those handcuffs. The little kinky fantasy with my oils was still pretty fresh in my head and I was trying to concentrate on teaching her.

The jewelry I made her was meant to come off easily. I showed her how to get the necklace off. I showed her the locking mechanism on a second pair of handcuffs. Picking a lock while your hands were chained together was difficult, even more so when they were cuffed to the back. I didn't do that to her the first time she tried.

I knew the girl was flexible from the dances she did for us, but she just laughed and told me she was double jointed too. She was able to turn her wrist in a way that she was able to get the bobby pin in the lock pretty easily, but actually getting the handcuffs unlocked proved much more difficult. I was trying to encourage her, but she was adorable biting her lower lip in concentration trying to get it open.

"I think I've just about—Yup, got it!" she said in triumph after unlocking the cuff from her left wrist. She looked so happy and I wanted to celebrate with her, but I also needed to prepare her. I needed to be like Milo and put my dick aside to prepare her for if she was handcuffed for real if Rook had her.

"Good. Now, remember this, Misty. It's important. You may only have time to pick one of the locks. You just need your hands free and if you have metal cuffs attached to one hand, they can be used as a weapon. If you punch someone with the hand with the cuffs still attached to it, it will do additional damage. I *only* want you doing that in extreme circumstance. If Rook has you, you don't pick your cuffs until you've already figured a way out of where he's hiding you. You don't pick your cuffs until your guard is gone or distracted. If your guard is armed, you do what you did to Jake. You wait until they leave their weapon unattended and pick the locks then. Whatever you do, don't shoot. Someone will hear and there might be someone else where they are keeping you. You beat them about the head with it until they are out, then you make your escape."

"You really think Rook is going to keep me somewhere with handcuffs? If he takes me, won't he just kill me like he did Aiden's grandmother?"

"I don't know why, but I don't think Rook intends to kill you right off. There's a bigger plan here we aren't seeing. If Rook really wanted Casey off his trail, Serena's bomb would have killed him. If Rook wanted this investigation to stop, he would kill Bishop and Leo. With Casey out of commission, that would derail this investigation. Without Leo and Bishop, Casey wouldn't know who to trust. No, something else is going on, I just don't know what."

"Why didn't you ever join the force like Casey, Gareth? You're smart and you look at the big picture. You've been such a huge asset in this investigation and I know Bishop wants you."

Misty didn't know because I'd never told her. It had nothing to do with Casey becoming a cop. I never talked about my family with Misty, but I could trust her.

"My dad was a cop and so was my grandfather. They both expected me to join the force. My parents are pretty boring. The follow the same routine every day. My dad was always trying to prep me for becoming a cop and my mom was always petrified something was going to happen to both of us. Everything I'm teaching you, my dad taught me. When I was just a kid and should have been out playing. I started resenting it. I'm not happy being a security guard and my father always talks down to me about it if I visit, but I know I don't want to be a cop. Casey didn't either when we were kids. He decided when we were in the military."

Misty got the other cuff off and dangled it from her finger. "What do you really want to do, Gareth?"

"I'll figure it out eventually. I know I don't want to be a cop, but I like computers and I like what Milo has been teaching me. You can't hack for a living and I'd be miserable fixing people's computers. I don't want to code like Andre either. I haven't really found anything I'd want to do the rest of my life."

Misty looked at me like she understood. "I like numbers and order, but I wasn't really happy at my job back in California. I stayed because I was good at it. Handling the business side of Aiden's shop and art seems like something that combines two things I love and would make me happy. The insurance adjuster I'm dealing with about the vandalism is a bit of a dick and I think he thinks he can get away with screwing Aiden over because he's an artist and I'm a woman. I bookmarked the Louisiana Department of Insurance website and I've already threatened him with it."

"Aiden is lucky you're doing this. Aside from when we were fighting over you, Aiden hates conflict and would have agreed to the first settlement offered."

"It's not just the conflict. Aiden showed me the murals on the shop walls and I have the receipts from all the equipment. The adjuster thinks I'm a huge pain in the ass, but I'm billing him for wages lost for both Aiden and Badger and the cost for the new paint on the walls."

I just chuckled. "Casey is so worried about being the big man and protecting you, but you fucked Jake up pretty badly and I suspect Rook isn't going to know what hit him if he gets his hands on you. You learned how to pick those cuffs pretty quickly. With practice, you'll be able to do it easier and faster."

Misty's gray eyes hooded and she looked at me like a cat. "I got out of the handcuffs. I believe you owe me a fantasy now."

"Anything you desire goes, Misty."

8

isty seemed shy, almost like our first day alone in my bedroom when I gave her a backrub to relax her. She was staring down at her hands like she didn't want to give voice to what she was going to ask me. I didn't speak. If she didn't want to play her game, we didn't have to. If she wanted to go back to the living room, we could do that too.

I realized she was staring down at my handcuffs. "Can I use these on you and just touch you? I want you to lie totally still and not do a thing while I explore your body. I want you to let me do whatever I want to you. Do you trust me?"

"I trust you and I love you. If you just want to touch me and do nothing else, you can do that, Misty. I want this game to be about what *you* want. I'm not going to judge you for anything you want to do."

Misty gave me this shy smile. "May I undress you?"

I stood up and stood totally still. I didn't understand

why Misty was being so shy after everything we'd done together. She could do whatever she wanted to me. Even kinky stuff I wouldn't have agreed to with anyone else, I'd do it just because she wanted to.

I lifted my arms to help her pull my shirt off. I stood totally still, practically holding my breath, as her hands trailed down my chest down my stomach. She walked behind me and I shivered as her hands traced the muscles on my back. She walked back in front of me and her hand trailed down my abs to my fly. I had no idea if she meant this to be erotic, but it was certainly turning me on.

I was hoping she didn't mind my erection when she gently pulled my pants down. I stepped out of them and I realized she didn't when her soft hand caressed my cock. I groaned and she let her hand make a trail around my hips to caress my ass. She cupped both cheeks with her hands and I felt her breasts press against my back. Her heart was racing and so was mine.

"Can you get on the bed, Gareth?"

"I'm yours to obey. I'll be your slave if you want." I crawled on the bed and lifted my hands to the headboard, nodding my head it was okay for her to handcuff me.

I felt the metal close around each wrist and Misty was straddling my chest. I closed my eyes as she stroked my face and hair. I could have done this all night. I turned my face towards her hand as she caressed my cheek. She ran her thumb across my bottom lip and I just wanted to nip at it, but I didn't.

"You're so beautiful, Gareth," she crooned.

"Not compared to you, Misty."

Her hands stroked their way down my neck and she snuggled into my chest. Her fingers brushed across my nipple and I groaned. We just stayed like that for a while. Her snuggled into me playing with my chest and nipples. When I felt her move, I wanted to pull her back, but my hands were cuffed and I promised not to.

I thought tonight was just going to be about touching, but I felt her long, red nails rake down my thighs. She hovered over my cock and I could feel her cool breath on me.

"You have such a beautiful body, Gareth. What do you do to stay in shape?"

She was so close. Her full lips were just inches away from my cock. I knew she wanted an answer, so I gave one. "I have a black belt in Krav Maga."

I didn't think it was possible for her to get any closer to my dick and not touch it, but she did. "Can you teach me how to defend myself?"

"I'll teach you whatever you want, Misty."

Her tongue flicked out and caressed the head of my cock. Jolts shot through me. That little lick was so erotic and left me panting. This whole fantasy, with her just touching me, was unusual for me, but I found out I really loved what she was doing. The feel of her hands exploring my muscles and letting her do whatever she wanted was a huge turn on. If that was all she intended with me for the day before she left to go back out to the others, it was enough for me, no matter how turned on I was.

Apparently, Misty had other plans. She wrapped her small hand around my cock and started giving my shaft slow, teasing licks.

"Your cock is beautiful too, Gareth. Nice and thick and the way it curves up does certain things to me."

No one had ever said anything like that to me. Some of the girls I brought home had filthy things to say about the size of my dick, but none had ever said anything like that while they were practically worshipping it with their tongue.

"What does it do to you?" I gasped. She was swirling her tongue around the head of my cock. She hadn't taken it in her mouth yet, but I was about to go off just from her tongue.

"It hits in all the right places. Let me show you how you make me feel."

I practically bucked on the bed when she finally did take me in her mouth. I had no idea simple touching as she had done would have turned me on this much.

"Misty, I'm going to ruin this fantasy of yours going off too soon if you keep doing that. I'm turned on as shit and I had no idea it would do that to me. I want you to feel good too."

She climbed back up and snuggled into my chest. My arms wanted to wrap around her and pull her close to me so I could smell her hair, but they were still chained to my headboard.

"Let's take a step back for a minute," she said, stroking my chest again. "I just wanted to explore your body. I thought you'd be bored."

"God, Misty, I don't think I've ever wanted you this much before. I love your fantasies."

"I also wanted to give you a little test, Gareth," Misty said, giving me this devious little smile. "If you can do this, then I can get myself out in whatever situation Rook manages to put me in."

"Oh?" I asked.

She pulled a bobby pin off her bracelet and leaned forward to put it in one of my hands. She slid down my cock and winked at me.

"Think you can get out of those like this?" she asked, slowly grinding into me.

Challenge accepted. I was getting out of these cuffs. I was aching to touch her after she touched me like that. She certainly wasn't making it easy. I could normally get out of handcuffs pretty easily, no matter if I was cuffed in front or back. My dad drilled that into me when I was just nine and wouldn't let me go play with my friends until I had it down.

Having my dad towering over me yelling at me as a child was hard, but having Misty riding my dick was almost impossible. My hands were shaking and fumbling as I tried to get the bobby pin in the lock. I shouldn't have alerted Misty when the bobby pin inserted into the lock because she just started riding me harder. I was having trouble concentrating, but I finally felt the familiar click of the lock and the cuff sprang open.

I didn't bother getting the second cuff off. I told Misty not to and I certainly wasn't about to when I had a beautiful woman riding my dick. When I was free, I sat up and pulled her to me. I knew how sensitive her collarbone was and I started nibbling on it. Her fingernails dug into my back and she sped up. I wasn't sure if she wanted me to touch her when I sat up, I just couldn't help it.

She apparently did because her hands tangled up in my hair and she pulled my face closer to her neck. If she wanted her neck kissed right then, I was going to do exactly what she wanted. This was her fantasy and I hoped I got to make more of them come true for her. I hoped she was close because I was about to go off any minute.

A jolt shot through my body and I couldn't help biting Misty's neck. That bite set everything off. Misty cried out and her pussy clamped down on my dick. I came like I'd had a ten-year dry spell after her hands touched me all over like that. We both clutched each other, our bodies shaking.

"Thank you, Gareth," Misty whispered. "I've always wanted to do that. I was afraid anyone I asked wouldn't enjoy it or think it was stupid."

"I'm never going to tell you anything you confide in me is stupid. Anything you say or we do in this room is between us. Any fantasy you tell me, I'll make it come true."

Misty cupped my face and kissed me gently. "I have a hard time believing you when you say you ever used to treat women the way you say."

I just kissed her back. I didn't want to think about how I used to be before I met Misty. I wanted to focus on the perfect woman I had now.

9
___

Misty and I joined the guys to sleep on the sectional. I had to get up early because Casey had a doctor's appointment to see if he was cleared for work. Before we left, Aiden checked him out. His bruises were now a wicked shade of green, but they weren't black and blue anymore. Casey was always a rotten patient and had issues staying still while Aiden examined him. Casey kept demanding to know if he was going to get cleared today.

I was just going as a bodyguard just in case anyone tried to hurt him. Our reasoning was that two of us were better than one and we had no idea who knew about Casey's appointment. I was dressed in a black button-down shirt and black slacks. I had a Kevlar vest on, a gun strapped to my chest under my jacket, and a taser in my pocket.

Casey needed to be cleared for work for us to grab Pete or else Leo would need to do it. Even with Leo doing it, Casey needed to be there to question Pete because Leo didn't know about Rook and he couldn't know yet. I could do it, but it would be better if both of us were there.

Casey wasn't fond of my driving and was already bitching when we got into my car. "Just don't get me injured more on the way there," he gruffed as he buckled his seatbelt.

"If you can handle Serena's bomb, you can handle my driving, jackass," I teased. One of my favorite things was riling Casey up.

"Just don't drive us into a building, Gareth. Can I put music on?"

I groaned. Casey's music was this depraved screaming and I always hated when he wanted to put his music on. "I swear, I'll drive slowly if you don't put your music on."

Casey always looked shocked when someone didn't like his music, but actually agreed with me because as much as I hated his music, he hated my driving equally. It always took a while to get into the city because our compound was pretty far away from everything. Driving with Casey was always complicated. You never knew if he wanted to just sit there in total silence or talk. He never said and if he was in the mood to brood and you tried to start a conversation, it would sour his mood. I had no idea if that had changed since Misty arrived since I hadn't been alone in the car with him.

Apparently, he wanted to talk. "Do you think Misty is going to eventually get sick of us and leave?"

"I hope not. I don't think so. I mean, she seems happy. I think things will be better once we get Rook and she has more freedom. It'll be awesome to take her out on dates."

"I want her to meet my mom, but I had to ask her to go stay with her sister in Boston. She doesn't know I'm hurt or she would have come to the house. She didn't understand why I asked her not to come to Granny's funeral party and she suspects I'm in deep trouble and that's why I asked her to leave New Orleans."

"Is Alice blowing up your phone?" I asked. Alice was more of a mother to me than my own was, same way Aiden's granny was my granny. Andre's mom was also another mother to me.

"You know it. I'm trying to fool her by not answering my phone like I'm at work, but you know her. She's going to figure it out and come barging back to Louisiana. I can't have something happen to my mom, Gareth. Not like Granny."

"It won't, Casey. If she comes back, she moves in with us. Plus, we have a mark now. Pete could give us something on Rook."

"Pete doesn't fit the profile. He's a seasoned cop. He became a cop before the internet was a thing. He wouldn't have met Rook through an online class. I find it hard to believe he was the one hacking Leo. Before he went on leave, he was still bitching about having to use a computer to submit his reports."

"Pete could have been bitching that loud about not wanting to use a computer to throw people off that he's hacking things on his downtime," I pointed out.

"No, you'd have to know Pete. He's kind of this bland, boring guy. I don't take him for someone who could act that well. And I don't take him for one of Rook's."

"Well, we're going to find out the truth soon enough," I said, pulling into the parking lot.

I stayed in the waiting room and texted with Misty while Casey was in the back getting checked out. We were both in work mode. Misty was telling me what was going on at the house and I was updating her on Casey. Andre was still digging into Pete and watching his computer. Misty and Andre thought something was off with Pete. They watched him try to get into Leo's computer. He'd used a VPN, but it looked like he wasn't some expert hacker. He'd managed to get into Leo's computer, but Misty texted he was slow about it, almost like he was checking instructions.

Casey needed to know this and he seemed to be taking forever in the back. We needed to get home and discuss this all together. Casey finally came out with a shit eating grin that faltered when he saw the look on my face. I would break the news after his.

I clapped him on the back. "I take it that grin was good news?"

"I'm cleared for light field work. Which means I can go with Leo to bust Pete without having to bring you to Bishop's attention again. I want you there for questioning. Leo is getting squirrely about doing everything under Bishop's nose and Bishop is starting to get demanding. Now, why were you looking like that when I came out?"

I slammed the car door. "Because you were right about Pete. Misty and Andre don't think he's that good with computers. I think he might be being blackmailed into being a knight or pawn."

"That's actually good news," Casey said, slamming his door. "Pete is a good cop. If he's being blackmailed, then he may give us Rook the easy way."

10

Bishop was apparently losing his shit that he had no idea what was going on. Casey was cleared for light field work, but still working from home planning Pete's bust. Leo wasn't talking either and getting pretty uncomfortable Bishop kept yelling at him. Casey was pretty hard on Leo too, yelling at him this had to be top secret, even from Bishop. I knew Casey hated keeping secrets from Bishop, but he hated losing to Rook.

We had a plan. I would pick up Milo and someone named Ziva Cox, who was active FBI. We would watch from a coffee shop until Casey and Leo grabbed Pete, then bring him to the office building Ziva set up for us. According to Milo, Ziva thought all of this was horse shit and a waste of her time, but we all knew better.

I was antsy the few days leading up to the bust. I was on edge and waiting for this. I knew I didn't want to be a cop, but the idea of busting Pete excited me. I couldn't wait to be a part of questioning him with Milo and Casey.

We tried to cover all our bases. I was going to meet Milo and Ziva at a coffee shop close to the grocery store Pete shopped at and we'd watch from a table across the street. Milo wasn't active FBI, but Ziva and Milo were going to be backup if Pete made a scene. We thought we prepared for everything this time. Between Ziva and Milo, there couldn't have been anything we missed this time.

When the time came, Casey left early, but Pete didn't shop until noon. It seemed like I was waiting for hours to go to the coffee shop. I tried pacing, playing around on the computer, and my hair was sticking up from running my fingers through it so much. The only thing that got my mind off things was that Casey turned his bodycam on so that we could watch him at the station.

Misty stretched herself across all our laps and we watched Casey get greeted by his coworkers then yelled at by Bishop. Bishop demanded a status update and I expected Casey to lose it. Casey just calmly said they had a mark and when he knew something, Bishop would.

It seemed like it had been days, but it was finally time for me to go to the coffee shop. Milo was sitting with a dark-skinned woman around my age. She was tall and muscular with a shaved head. She looked like a supermodel, but I could tell she was also damned good at her job. She was eyeing her surroundings and didn't miss a thing. She noticed me before Milo did and already seemed to know who I was. Ziva gave me a subtle nod and focused back on Milo.

She was all business when I sat down. I knew I couldn't crack any jokes and ruin this. Or at least I thought I couldn't. Milo acted like his usual self when I sat down.

"Ziva, this is Gareth. He's going to help us question the shit stain before he grabs his Ex-Lax and prunes."

I couldn't help my grin. I'd seen Pete's shopping list too. Ziva just rolled her eyes. "I'm aware of this and I don't need the man's shopping habits. What we need to be doing is watching the door in case your boys get into trouble."

Maybe she *didn't* have all the details. "He's recovering from back surgery, so he's got a parking tag. Leo and Casey already knew what car he drives. They are going to grab him as soon as he parks."

Ziva raised one perfectly sculpted eyebrow at me, but before she had a chance, Milo practically slammed his coffee cup down.

"We're in business. A blue Buick is pulling into the store now. Fairly sure that's him. Your boys look ready to pounce."

Sure enough, it was Pete. Casey and Leo didn't even let him open the door. I saw them from across the street as they knocked on the window. Pete rolled it down and I could see the color drain from his face from where I was. He didn't put up a fight. He must have asked to move his car because Leo got in and parked it in another spot. They didn't cuff him, they just walked him to the back of Leo's squad car and Pete obediently got in.

"That's our cue," Milo said, standing up. "Hope you

didn't want coffee, Gareth. The coffee where we're going will burn a hole in your stomach."

I was good. I wanted to get to that office and see if Pete could give us Rook. It wasn't that far from the store and looked like a totally benign building. It was a glass building that appeared to have several floors dedicated to various offices. I followed Milo and Ziva to the elevator, thinking we were going up. I was surprised when Ziva entered a key and pressed the down button.

"How do you keep something underground here when it floods? We constantly have hurricanes here and we don't have basements. Hell, we can't even bury people underground because if it floods, coffins start floating down the street," I asked.

Ziva must not have been from New Orleans. "I'm really not in the mood for more New Orleans urban legends. If you're trying to get me to go to a haunted graveyard tour, you're wasting your time," she snapped.

"Stay away from the tours, but Gareth isn't bullshitting you about the coffins. Gareth, they took precautions building underground here. It's watertight, even if the building takes water."

I wanted a detailed explanation on how they managed that because you just *did not* build underground in New Orleans, but the elevator ride was short and I was bustled into a room with a two-way mirror. They finally decided to put handcuffs on Pete and he was cuffed to the table. The man just looked old and weary. I knew whatever Casey was going to ask him about Rook would be after he managed to get Leo on the room, but Casey seemed to be letting Leo lead the questioning.

"Want to tell me why you've been poking around in my computer and poisoning cops?"

Pete just sighed. I had no idea if we were going to have to rough him up to get him to talk, but he seemed perfectly willing to spill the beans.

"If I tell you, can you keep me away from her? Can you keep me safe?"

"Her?" Leo asked. "If you help us, we'll protect you. Who do you mean by *her*?"

"You both know full well who I'm talking about. I thought you were going to get her out my hair, but apparently, that little bitch also knows how to build a bomb. She ruined my life."

I watched the gears turning in Casey's head. Now would be the time to ask Leo to leave, but there was no way to get him out of there now that Pete was willingly talking. Casey folded his fingers and calmly looked at Pete. His face never betrayed him that he knew Serena wasn't the lone wolf pulling strings.

"You're a good cop, Pete. How did Serena get to you?"

Pete hung his head. "My wife was cheating on me. She was mad at me because I was never home. Or at least, that was what I thought. Serena claimed she had been seeing her on her beat outside the motel. She had photos of my wife with another man. She acted like she was there for me at first. She asked me out to a bar just to forget about my wife for one night. I have no idea what happened. She must have slipped something in my drink. I woke up in her house naked next to her in bed. She told me she videotaped the entire thing. She said I'd have to do whatever she asked after that, but I haven't killed any cops, I swear. If she asked me to do that, I would have come clean to my wife. The photos Serena showed me were photoshopped. If I hadn't been so upset, I would have noticed."

"And what did Serena ask you to do? Did she mention anyone else?" Casey asked. I could practically see fire dancing in his blue eyes. The same was probably in mine. Pete probably didn't know a damned thing about Rook.

"She didn't ask me for a damned thing for the longest time, but she did like to gloat. She'd try to get me alone, touch my crotch, and tell me it belonged to her. I thought she was just fucked in the head and was playing games with me. Someone I'm close with at the station, they don't know what she did to me, but I've always suspected I wasn't the only one. They knew I didn't like her, but they never knew why. They called to tell me they were going to be pounding on her door and bringing her in. Her bomb killed several good men.

"I thought she would go on the run after that. When she told me I was hers now, she gave me a phone. She told me to keep it on me at all times and if she needed me, she'd contact me on it. I just put the phone in a drawer and ignored it after she killed several officers. She showed up *at my house* while I was recovering from back surgery. She had a computer and a smartphone with her.

"She sat in my living room the entire night demanding to know what my exact schedule was. I knew what she was doing. She was putting me on a leash. She wanted to know where I was at all hours. I didn't get any sleep that night because she put all these doodads on the computer and demanded I start watching Leo and Bishop. I was supposed to run this program any time I looked and I was ordered to get the phone out of the drawer and use it. I was supposed to report any names on Leo and Bishop's files to her."

Leo and Casey both looked like they thought Pete was full of shit. *I* thought Pete was full of shit. He said he wasn't responsible for the death of a cop, but if he had been in the loop about Serena, someone would have told him about Grant. Leo brought that up before Casey could. I could tell Casey was still trying to keep his temper in check over Granny.

"Let me try to make sense of this, Pete," Leo said through gritted teeth. "You claim Serena is blackmailing you over a tape and you would have come clean if she asked you to kill a cop. One of the names you gave her from *my* files was poisoned in his jail cell after promising to give us the names of more corrupt cops. You *did* kill a cop. A dirty cop, but you do have blood on your hands. Grant Winder ring a bell?"

Pete's brows furrowed. "I never gave her that name. Serena only showed up at my house a few days ago. You caught me after I got into Leo's computer only a few times. I never saw anything in his files about a cop to give her."

Pete looked utterly bewildered and a little ashamed he'd be trapped by Serena, but he was adamant he wasn't the one who gave her Grant. And we still hadn't found anything out about Rook.

"Leo, can you step outside and get us food from the deli on the first floor?" Casey asked.

Good. We could finally get down to Rook business.

Leo scowled like he didn't want to be the errand boy, but he finally disappeared. Casey just sat there, studying Pete until he was sure Leo was gone.

"Was anyone with Serena when she visited you or did she mention anyone else she was working with?"

"She did threaten me with her boyfriend. She said the computer and the phone came from him and if I didn't put them to good use, I'd have more to worry about than my back and that tape. I don't know much about gadgets, but the phone and the computer seemed expensive. She did say something that gave me pause. She said if I ever talked about anything she said or anything she asked me to do, no one on the planet could keep me safe. She said someone would find me anywhere I tried to run."

I was about to get up and start pacing. We *still* didn't have Rook. But, apparently, we got the attention of the FBI. Ziva pulled her phone out of her pocket and started barking out orders. In the span of five minutes, she arranged for someone to go to Pete's house and get his family and she arranged a safe house she didn't even say the location out loud so I could hear.

Ziva hung up and rested her elbows on her knees, focusing on the two-way mirror. Casey wasn't done with Pete yet.

"If she threatened you like that, why are you talking now?"

Pete sighed. "I'm getting old, Sullivan. There's a damned good chance when I'm cleared to go back to work, they are going to stick me at a desk hoping I retire. If Serena's boyfriend really exists and he's got cops at his disposal, I don't want to stay at my job with dirty cops.

Serena was stupid for targeting me. As soon as I figured out why she wanted names from Leo's files, I would have cracked. I only did what she asked to figure out what she was up to."

"Well, you got yourself in deeper shit than just Serena's blackmail. She wasn't joking when she told you her boyfriend has connections. When we brought you here, we thought you were the one that gave her Grant's name. Grant was working with Serena and her boyfriend too. Committed murder and got caught. He was going to talk and this was something just between Leo and me. Someone close to Serena and her boyfriend found out and he was poisoned in his cell. Do you see how deep the shit you've gotten into is?"

"My wife—" Pete said, finally looking panicked.

Ziva was out the door and into the interrogation room in seconds. Leo came in right behind her carrying a bag of food. Apparently, Leo wasn't clued in the FBI was watching, nor the fact that Milo and I were there. I don't know who was shocked to see the three of us in the room more, Pete or Leo.

Ziva didn't hesitate to whip out her badge. She informed Pete both he and his wife were being moved to a safe house and that she would be bringing in a local agent to work with her and all of us on this case. Casey seemed relieved he was getting help, but Leo seemed furious.

"So, that's it? You're just swooping in and taking this from us? How did you even find out and what does the FBI want with a few bad cops at our precinct?"

"Leo, sit down," Casey said. "You need to hear the full truth away from any ears at the station. This *cannot* leave this room, not even to Bishop just yet. If Bishop asks, we're looking at Serena. No one can know about this until we have an identity. I didn't tell you before because we were shooting at nothing and it was for your safety. If you want out of this for your family, tell me now."

"Exactly what have you gotten me into, Sullivan?" Leo demanded. "It's a little too late to back out now if someone is getting shit off my computer."

"We can move your family too," Ziva said. "Just say the word."

"Where the hell was the FBI when Serena was planting bombs and cops were getting poisoning in their cells?" Leo yelled.

"Casey hadn't met me yet, son," Milo said. "Calm your tits. I was dating the woman Grant killed and *I* got the FBI involved because I used to work for them. The shit you boys have stumbled into is almost so ridiculous, the FBI didn't believe me at first. Ziva heard Pete's story and now she wants to get involved. She's not stealing your case because it'll tip this Rook off if he sees her at the station. Casey will be sharing what he finds with her while we come up with a plan."

"Who the fuck is Rook?" Leo yelled.

"I'd like to know that too," Pete said, looking upset.

"He's a cop or politician playing a chess game with cops. Jake and Dillion were his men and Serena is his lover and queen. Most of the people he's targeted have been young or have been working for him for a long time. Pete, you don't fit his usual profile and he had to have known it would be a risk to try to bring you to their side. It doesn't make sense."

"I think Pete is a diversion," Ziva said. "Rook probably let Serena bring Pete in as a backup plan. That was why she hasn't asked him to do anything so far. Milo tells me you've caught everyone Rook has tried to use to hack anyone. Pete is either a test to see if hacking the way Serena taught him to do it is successful or they want us looking at Pete while they are doing something more sinister."

"It's more than that now that I think about it," Pete said. "Ten years ago, before I moved to homicide, I busted a cop for serial rape. Last I heard, he got transferred, but he could have been one of this Rook's men."

"More than likely," Casey said. "The men who kidnapped my girlfriend were both his men and one escaped a transport and the other managed to walk out a locked prison. It wouldn't shock me if he was one of Rook's and is no longer in prison."

I had my phone out furiously texting Andre. "Give me his name and I'll find out."

"Ashton Roth. I'll never forget that man," Pete said. "I thought he was my friend and answered honestly when he would ask about my investigation into the rapes. He almost got away with it, but he let a woman get away and she saw his face. The woman saw him at the station and that was that."

I noticed Ziva was texting like a mad woman too. "Your wife is safe. Any kids or grandkids we need to worry about?"

"No. She never wanted to because of my job."

"I'll take you to your wife. I don't agree this was revenge for Ashton. It doesn't make sense. If these people were willing to kill Milo's girlfriend and vandalize the shop of her grandson when he wasn't even involved with Serena getting caught, it would make more sense for Pete to die in the line of duty than this."

"I think Rook was much more careful before he took up with Serena," I pointed out. "You should see the footage from the night they trashed Aiden's shop. Even without knowing about the bomb, just that video shows she's totally unstable."

Ziva gave me a curt nod. "I'll be working with Agent Eckart on this. I want everything you have, sent through encrypted servers from computers Rook and Serena know nothing about. *No one* outside this room needs to know the FBI is involved. I don't care how high up on the food chain they are at your precinct or what demands they make of you. *Nothing* is said about the FBI unless it's from phones we give you and no one outside this room. Is this understood?"

Leo looked like he was about to shit himself, but got himself under control. Milo gave me this sly wink as he was leaving. That crabby old man delivered on his promise.

It may take a while, but we had the FBI on our side now.

11

I couldn't say I was shocked the living room was empty when I got home and Andre, Misty, and Aiden didn't reappear until breakfast. They already knew we had the FBI on our sides and Aiden's mood appeared to be slightly better when they finally did join us. Misty and Andre immediately set to their routine of playing and cooking. I wasn't jealous this time. I knew how much Andre liked cooking and it was nice to see Misty dancing around him and swatting at him with pot holders. He looked like he was having the time of his life and I had my own thing with Misty now.

We pretending like everything was normal over breakfast, laughing and cracking jokes. We took our time eating for once because we knew we had Ziva helping us. Maybe it was false security, but I think we just needed an hour that morning now that we had help to pretend like after Misty helped us find her after Jake took her, all of this was over and we were all safe.

It was only maybe an hour, but it brightened our

moods. There was a delivery person at the gate when we finished. We had to be careful letting anyone through it now and no one was expecting a package. We buzzed him through when we realized the package was from Ziva. It was actually several boxes. I had no idea what Milo told her, but there were five computers and five phones in there. Ziva sent computers and phones for Misty and Aiden too.

"What the fuck am I supposed to do with this?" Aiden asked, scowling at the laptop and phone in his hand. "I'm not a part of the investigation."

"You are now," Misty said, playing with his long hair like she was doing all the time now that Granny was gone. "So am I. You have information on Granny and your shop and I have information on Jake. We don't have to be hackers, computer experts, or cops. I know Jake and if you talk to Ziva, she can figure out why you were targeted."

It didn't take long for Misty's computer to start sounding off some sort of alert. There was some sort of video chat program installed I wasn't familiar with. Misty figured out how to answer it pretty quickly and her monitor split with two webcams. Ziva was there and the other agent had to be Eckart.

"Nice to meet you, Miss Hardwin. Since this started with you, I wanted to talk to you first. From what I understand, Jake targeted you without an order from Rook. Why would he disobey?"

"Well, Jake is in California and Rook has to be based here if his lover is. We know Jake met Rook and Dillion on that online class, but I would imagine Jake wasn't as scared of Rook as the cops in Louisiana because he was just too far away and didn't think he would find out about trying to get my trust fund."

Ziva just laughed. "Jake clearly underestimated what was right under his nose. I've already got copies of all his medical records of what you did to him. Why New Orleans, Misty? It seems like a *huge* coincidence you fled Jake and just happened to end up in a heavily fortified house with a cop and two hackers. A cop who just happens to be working at the same precinct as several of Rook's players."

I already knew where Ziva was headed with this and I wanted to defend my woman. Casey, Aiden, and Andre were starting to get riled up too. Misty was furious.

"I'm *not* working for Rook!" she yelled. "I came to New Orleans because it was Mardi Gras and I hoped to hide among the tourist. I was going to tell Aiden no when he asked me to stay here. How can you think I could sit here talking to Aiden after what those animals did to his shop and grandmother? I'm helping Aiden with the vandalism that was done to his shop!"

Misty was pissed and Ziva never lost her cool. "I wasn't suggesting you were one of Rook's. I asked why New Orleans. You fled Jake and appear to have landed in the jaws of a lion. I simply asked why New Orleans."

"I'm not a hacker and at the time, I had no idea Jake killed my father. Are you suggesting I somehow should have known I was running to Jake's boss?"

"I'm just trying to figure you out, Miss Hardwin. I think everything happens for a reason. Maybe luck is something I don't believe in, but maybe it *was* luck that brought you here to expose all this. Why were you going to tell Aiden no, but you ended up at that house anyway? Aiden looks like a big, sexy guy. Why would you say no to that?"

Misty gave an epic eyeroll. "I'm not dumb enough to trust someone just because they look like Aiden. They brought me back here because I didn't realize how strong the drinks were where we were drinking and I couldn't tell them no. If I hadn't been passed out, you wouldn't even be here right now and neither would I!"

Ziva finally nodded like she wasn't poking Misty hoping she would slip. "Yes, I've noticed the drinks here are certainly not watered down. I'm going to need your help, Miss Hardwin. Rook's game started unraveling with Jake. As far as we know, Rook has never sacrificed one of his pieces before and he started with Jake and Dillion. We need to know what was so important about Jake that he would start losing pieces on his board. Especially someone Misty was able to take down so easily with no training."

"Jake sold his soul to the devil once. Rook probably knew he'd sell him out and every player he knew about just to save his own hide. Jake couldn't have gotten to me without help. I can only guess Rook threatened Jake and Jake threatened Rook. I think Dillion was told to sacrifice himself to make Jake happy and get him out of Rook's hair, then Dillion was promised Rook would get him out. And Rook got both Jake and Dillion out. We have no idea where they are now."

"Maybe, maybe not," Eckart said, finally speaking. "Serena told Pete if anyone came asking questions, to put them off, dispose of the computer, and she gave him an address and told him to go there. Pete let that slip after I asked him to go over everything Serena told him that he might have forgotten. We're going to assign men to watch that house. May I speak to Aiden next, please?"

"Not if you're going to accuse him of shit the way you did me!" Misty snapped.

Ziva finally cracked a smile. I had no idea if she knew about our unconventional relationship or what Milo had told her about the five of us. "No, I suspect I'd have both you and Milo coming for my head if I said the wrong thing to Aiden."

"What do you want?" Aiden asked, sitting next to Misty where Ziva and Eckart could see him.

"To assure you we will get Rook. Your grandmother was dating Milo and that makes her a part of our family. Rook and Serena will pay for what they did to Clara and your shop. We have more resources than all of you had before, but we need to be working together. Now, we have the location of a possible safe house, but Gareth and Casey don't think Serena is there. Casey and Misty know our list of suspects the best. All of you have been watching them. What are the chances Serena and Rook end up at that house?"

"None. We think they've been communicating by burner phones," Casey said. "Pete kind of disrupted that theory since Serena gave him an iPhone."

Pete's phone had me thinking too. We all just assumed they were using prepaid phones with no cellular connection.

"What if they are all using iPhones so Rook can monitor their locations and texts? Have you dug into Pete's Mac and iPhone yet?"

"They were collected as evidence and are being gone through. Milo tells me you and Andre are quite adept at getting into things you shouldn't, but understand, if you want Rook and Serena to pay, we need *legally* obtained evidence," Eckart pointed out.

Ziva gave us this devious grin. "I'm not telling you to stop looking. If you find something, I can also find it the legal way. Do you understand me?"

Andre and I both grinned. I think we had both assumed we would be sidelined and Casey would be working with the FBI. Ziva basically just gave us permission to poke around where we wanted for this investigation.

"Can I get my hands on Pete's iPhone?" Andre asked.

Ziva was still grinning. "You didn't get his cloud account when you got in there the first time?"

"Yeah, but this is an Apple-free household," I pointed out. Even Misty, who was a new addition to the house didn't have Apple products. The phones Ziva shipped us weren't Apple either. They were some sort of military grade smartphone.

Ziva just shrugged. "If you have Pete's cloud account and password, then I suggest you make an exception and bring one into the house because there's no way in hell you're getting your hands on evidence. And if anyone tries to hack it while it's in evidence, you'd better make damned sure it's not you. I don't care how good you think you are, we will know and I'll boot you out this investigation so fast my heel will leave a permanent dent in your ass."

My mouth was starting to do that thing again that got me in trouble. "Yes, mom," I said, holding up my pinky.

"Take a day off from all of this," Ziva said. "You have

help now and we won't know anything until we've watched the address Pete gave us. I've got no idea what the five of you do to relax, but just take a day to do it. I'll be in touch."

The call disconnected and we all just looked around at each other. Even our time alone and together with Misty was focused on Rook. It had been this all-consuming thing and Rook had taken something from all of us except me and Andre. I don't think any of us knew what to do with an entire Rook free day. Our conversation with Ziva and Eckart hadn't taken long at all. Could we possibly have the majority of the day to not deal with Rook shit? Could we actually spend the entire day not thinking about him?

"All of you need a break now that we have help," Misty said, standing up. "He said he didn't want to celebrate, but Aiden's birthday is coming up. Aiden, the FBI can be a present you didn't know you were getting. Can I make you a cake and we celebrate?"

I saw the first smile from Aiden since Bishop broke the news about Granny like a total shit stain. "Yeah, I think I'd like that, Misty."

Misty hopped in his lap and kissed him. "What's your favorite cake?"

"Doberge cake," I said since I knew Aiden wouldn't. "It's a New Orleans thing and Andre would be happy to help you make it. Aiden and I will watch his favorite movie while the two of you cook."

Aiden had always loved Granny's Doberge cake and Andre learned to make that cake from her. We all knew it was his favorite and that Misty would have had no idea how to make it. He would have said something, anything other than his favorite because he knew it would have been easier for her to make it.

This was the better solution. Misty loved cooking with Andre and they would both have fun in the kitchen. None of us liked Aiden's movies and wouldn't watch them with him. It would mean a lot to Aiden for Casey and me to just let him pick a movie and sit there watching it with him because we never did that.

And I felt like a rotten friend because with all this Rook business, I had forgotten Aiden's birthday.

12

Casey and I just sat back and let Aiden pick the movie. That huge sentimental bastard had a thing for Disney and Pixar movies. I liked dark foreign films and crabby ass Casey didn't like to sit still long enough to enjoy the beauty of a movie. I thought Aiden was going to put on some tear jerker where Bambi's mother died or some shit, but I was shocked when he put on one of the more upbeat Disney movies. Maybe he would actually enjoy his birthday today.

I already knew Misty and Andre would be in the kitchen a while. Granny was famous for her Doberge cake and wouldn't be caught dead serving anything less than eight layers, custard from scratch for the layers, and Granny's cake used buttercream *and* a fondant glaze to finish it off. Aiden's favorite was the traditional half lemon and half chocolate. Granny loved all of us, but she loved Aiden best. When Andre asked her to teach him her recipe, she made all of us learn so someone would always be able to make her grandbaby his favorite.

When Granny talked, you paid attention, even if learning to bake a cake wasn't something you were interested in. I could have easily gone in there and helped Misty and Aiden with that cake, but this was their time together and Aiden needed me, even if it was just to sit next to him and watch this musical.

I was starting to get worried about what was going on in the kitchen when Aiden started yet another movie. The cake should have been done. We all turned around when someone dimmed the lights. I knew it was supposed to be Aiden's birthday, but I'll be damned if I didn't wish it was mine when Misty came out carrying the cake wearing nothing but fuck me heels and had tied a bow around her neck. Aiden's mouth was hanging open right along with me and Casey's.

My birthday happened before Misty got here, but I was hoping this wasn't just a one-time performance. Misty sliced Aiden cake, then sat naked in his lap in just those six-inch heels feeding it to him. For someone who didn't want to celebrate his birthday, Aiden was certainly perking up.

"You nailed the cake, Misty," Aiden said, nuzzling her neck. "Are you going to have some?"

"After the birthday boy."

I loved Granny's Doberge cake too, but I'd certainly never eaten it like that. And when Aiden sliced a piece, started feeding Misty, and she was making those little contented noises at how good it was? I was starting to wish I learned to cook from a five-star chef and Granny like Andre had just to hear those noises from her. And it'd be nice to do something for Misty other than teach her to escape from bad men. She'd done so much for all of us and I couldn't even cook her favorite meal for her.

Aiden set the plate aside and the gentle look that used to be in his eyes before Granny was poking through. He stroked her bottom lip with his thumb.

"What are we going to do with you, Misty? You're going to run yourself ragged trying to take care of all of us. I don't want to run you off because you get tired of dealing with all our shit."

"Aiden, you think you aren't taking care of me too? Do all of you think this? Do you know what it was like for me before I came here? Even two hours away, I was always looking over my shoulder for Jake. My ex, the one you all hate, I don't think he wanted me to go to New York with him because he loved me. He wanted to marry me because my stock portfolio would have added to his. Don't you all understand? Even with all this Rook shit, I'm safe and there's so much love here. You all help me just as much as I try to do things for you. You just need to get used to a woman in the house with all of you that doesn't treat you like utter shit."

Casey and I didn't say a word. Andre didn't either. Casey and I did our fair share of treating women like shit and Andre was a total snob. Andre had totally ghosted girls for shit like he thought they had bad manners. Hell, I thought part of the reason Andre built this house like a fortress and invited us was the number of women the three of us pissed off. I think we all knew over dinner that first night Misty was going to be different.

Big, sappy Aiden looked like he was about to burst

into tears because out of all of us, he was probably the one who had been hurt the most instead of doing all the hurting. I think Misty could tell, so she changed gears. I had no idea why Aiden wanted to get all emotional with naked Misty in his lap in those heels, but he probably needed it. He was probably constipated from holding all that in since Granny.

"Aiden, I have another gift for you in my bedroom, but are you going to unwrap the one in your lap?" she purred, tilting her head a little so he could see the red bow around her neck that matched her red fuck me heels.

Aiden slowly untied that bow and let it fall on the couch. "It's my birthday celebration, so I want to do this my way. Misty says she feels loved here. I want all of us to show her *exactly* how much we love her."

None of us had to be asked twice to do that. Misty may have just wanted to cheer Aiden up and celebrate his birthday, but she was going to have a hell of a day.

13

We were all out of our clothes in seconds except for Andre. Andre just left and I had no idea what the hell was wrong with him until he came back with a leather bag. I still had no idea what Andre was doing until he started pulling all these toys out the bag. He had like, the Mary Poppins bag of sex toys if she was some sort of dominatrix instead of a nanny. Why hadn't I thought to get a few toys with Misty?

He brought out some sort of wand thing that looked like you could beat someone to death with it. He winked at Misty. "I always keep your favorite fully charged. Let's see how much you scream when I use it on you with the four of us."

It briefly flashed through my head that *I* should know Misty's favorite toy too, but I put that thought away. Andre had his toys and I had Misty's secret fantasies. She was still wrapped up in Aiden's lap and hadn't gotten herself settled so Andre could use that toy. She kissed Aiden deeply.

"It's your birthday and I'm one of your presents. How do you want to do this?"

Aiden gave this wicked smile and I was starting to wonder if Misty had any idea what she was getting herself into. One thing I had learned since Misty got here was that all my friends, even Casey, were a bunch of kinky fucks and now Andre just brought out toys into the mix.

"Is there lube in that bag?" Aiden asked.

Andre had apparently prepared for the fucking sexual apocalypse in that bag and pulled out three different kinds of lube. I didn't even want to ask what he was doing with the strawberry warming lube and that wasn't what Aiden wanted either. He still hadn't told us exactly how he was wanting to do this, but I was a little jealous when he handed Casey the lube instead of me.

Aiden just chuckled. "Well, I had no idea I'd be celebrating my birthday today, but I have an idea. Misty, slide that perfect ass of yours down Casey's dick."

"Why do I feel like all of you are going to be peeling me off the ceiling?" Misty laughed, crawling over to Casey.

"Oh, I fully plan on leaving you a quivering mess today, Misty. Andre bringing out his secret stash just gave me an idea."

Casey was groaning and it was hot as hell watching Misty work Casey's dick in her ass. Once she was settled, Casey wrapped his arms around her waist and started kissing her neck. Aiden finally motioned for me to join them. Aiden took her little perky breast, but I already knew what I wanted. Her collarbone was a huge sensitive spot for her and I start nibbling and kissing it.

I heard the noise of Andre's toy start and when he touched it to her clit, she must have jumped fifty feet and let out a shriek. Aiden definitely had a good idea and Andre's little black bag was full of surprises. Misty's entire body was shaking and we were all having trouble holding on to her. That toy didn't take long at all. Maybe that was why Andre said it was her favorite. Either that or the fact that it made her let out a huge shriek when her orgasm hit her.

I heard the toy turn off and Andre didn't waste any time at all. Almost as soon as the toy was off, he buried his face in her pussy and started licking her. I was giving her collarbones the attention they deserved while my friends took care of the rest of her. She couldn't decide whose name she wanted to scream out, so she just alternated when one of us did something she liked. She screamed mine every time I bit down on her collarbone.

Andre had her worked up again and it didn't take long for her to come again. She just sat in Casey's lap and held up her hand.

"Give me a minute to recover, then I think it's the birthday boy's turn. I want you inside me, Aiden."

Aiden was still all over her breasts. "What the lady wants, the lady gets."

We just sat there for a while, Casey kissing her neck from behind while buried in her ass, Aiden giving her breasts attention, and me with that collarbone of hers. She was giving these little contented sighs and moans that I think were driving all of us crazy.

"I want you, Aiden," she gasped.

Aiden grabbed her legs and slung them over his shoulder. Aiden and Casey both started thrusting into her. Andre took Aiden's spot and we were trying to give her pleasure in other places than where Casey and Aiden were. My dick was starting to ache when Misty's hand went between her legs to work her clit and she made those little noises I loved so much.

I watched all of the tension Aiden had been holding onto melt away as he fucked Misty. I was glad she got him to do this. Even if it didn't end with all of us together on the sectional, it was nice to see that haunted look out my buddy's eyes and his shoulder's straight instead of stooped. Things were definitely looking up for us and we had Milo to thank for that and this break from Rook.

Watching Misty finger herself with Aiden and Casey working her was seriously turning me on. Misty asked for another break after Casey and Aiden had her screaming. When she was ready again, she caressed my cheek, but she looked to Andre. What was that about?

"Do you remember that day Casey walked in on us?" she asked Andre.

I had no idea what the fuck they were talking about, but Andre scooped her up like she was a toy. He hooked her legs over his shoulders and I watched him slide into her. She turned her head as much as she could to glance at me.

"Care to join us, Gareth?"

She didn't have to ask me twice. I'd never had sex with her standing up because of our height difference, but Andre was showing me all kinds of things I'd never thought to do with her. I grabbed the lube before I got up from the couch, prepared myself, and came up behind Misty. She snaked an arm behind her to wrap around my neck as I slid into her ass.

Andre and I were around the same height of six foot two so she fit perfectly between us. Andre had his arms supporting her under her knees and I had my arms around her waist. She was totally secure like this, but she seemed to trust us not to drop her. Her nails dug into my neck as Andre and I bounced her on our cocks. Andre had her pretty securely, so I reached between the two of them and started fingering her clit.

"Oh, fuck!" Misty yelled as she came.

I felt her little ass flutter as she came and it set me off. I bit her shoulder as I came in her ass. Andre wasn't that far behind me. We both had to steady her when we set her down because her legs were shaking. I heard a chuckle from the sectional. Both Casey and Aiden were sitting there stroking their cocks.

"Hope you're in for a long day, little Misty," Casey growled.

14

When Ziva told us to take a break, she meant a four-day break. We still watched Leo and Bishop's computers to see if someone was trying to get in, but it was like watching paint dry. Casey was still working from home, even though he was cleared for light work, but there wasn't much for us to do. No one had tried to get back into Leo or Bishop's computers and we would have just been sitting there with our thumbs up our asses not knowing what was going on if it weren't for Ziva and Eckert.

Well, I would be lying to say we were sitting around doing nothing. We were still watching Leo and Bishop's computer and Misty was a fast learner. When I managed to get her away from everyone, we were still working on how to use the jewelry I made her. She could get out of the handcuffs with minimal effort now, so I started cuffing her behind her back. That was what we were working on now.

That little vixen gave me a fantasy every time. Some

were tame, something she just wanted to try, and some were more elaborate like how using my oils had been. We'd snuggle when we were done, but not as long as I would have liked to hold her. We were all being naughty now that the FBI took some of the Rook burden off our shoulders and flat out told us to do nothing except watch computers until we were given orders.

We just decided to keep up doing what we did on Aiden's birthday—show Misty how much we loved her. Andre was cooking huge, gourmet meals for her, I was giving her massages as often as I could get my hands on her, and Aiden finally started painting again. We were all so glad Aiden was picking up his art supplies again, none of us said a word to ruin it.

It was Casey that shocked me the most. Casey got into the most trouble out of all us growing up and almost got kicked out of school several times. I *never* took him for a literary lover, but that brooding shit was actually bringing out poetry and reading it to Misty. He wanted to show her his favorites.

We got naughty too, of course. We were so intent on pleasing her, she was having to ask for breaks. I think Aiden's words at his birthday hit us all and had been in the back of all our minds. None of us wanted Misty to think we were some burden because we all had our issues and have her leave because she got sick of our shit. We all probably went a little overboard, we were just all desperate not to ruin this.

Ziva, Eckart, and Milo finally had something for us on the fifth day. They called Casey on the laptop they gave him and we all crowded around it.

"We've been watching Pete's house and the address

he gave us. Can I tell you boys this and you not lose your shit and tip off Rook?" Ziva said.

"What is it?" Casey growled, pulling Misty protectively in his lap.

"We still don't have Serena or Rook. When Pete didn't check in with her, another man broke into his house. Dillion and Jake are holed up at the address Pete gave us. It's this large, ten-bedroom house, but they are the only ones staying there. They use a delivery service for groceries and never leave, but we've spotted both of them answering the door."

"And you're talking to us instead of arresting them why?" I demanded.

"This is where you boys need to look at the bigger picture. Serena and Rook didn't know what happened to Pete, so they sent someone else to his house to ransack it. We made it look like Pete and his wife left in a hurry, so they think Pete just ran. This is what we want. We have to leave Jake and Dillion at that house. They aren't leaving and they aren't a danger to Misty right now.

"If we swoop in and bust them, Serena and Rook are going to know the FBI is involved. They *can't* know until we arrest them. We need to be ahead of Rook for now. Pete is going to be our ace. We need to see what Rook does when someone runs."

"It would help if we had access to Pete's phone. I ordered an iPhone and signed into Pete's iCloud account, but there was no backup," Andre pointed out.

Something wasn't sitting right with me. I didn't have iPhone's mainly because I didn't like Apple or their policies, but if Rook was giving out iPhones, we should have Rook.

"Wouldn't the man Rook sent to Pete's house notice he took the iPhone and use it to track him? If they saw Pete disabled any tracking, they'd know he had help because Pete flat out admits he doesn't know how to use technology." They were keeping something from us and I didn't like it.

Ziva just grinned. "Pete is sort of the sacrificial lamb without us putting him on the table. Eckart is here because he could probably teach you boys a few things about hacking."

Eckart's dark eyes were sparkling. "As soon as they log in to Pete's account to check his location, I'll have theirs. And they will think Pete is in Guatemala because I've tricked the system."

"We could still help and use access to that phone. I haven't enabled any cloud services on it so they won't know and I immediately signed out," Andre said. "How will you know it's Serena and Rook who log in?"

"We won't until we watch. And that's *all* we're doing right now. No one can know the FBI is involved until we have everything in place to arrest Rook and Serena. No bombs this time."

Casey was rubbing his chin. He seemed to always have this five o'clock shadow now. "What of the man at Pete's house? Who is it?"

Ziva started flipping through a file. "Marcus Hastings. A detective. I was getting to that. Do you know him?"

"Yeah, Leo and I worked with him several years ago on a serial killer case. I didn't like him then and I like him less now. Do we actually have a plan where Leo and I actually do something?"

Casey was gritting his teeth. I knew what his problem was and it was mine too. Casey needed to be doing something right now and so did I. For some reason, I found myself rethinking my firm belief that I never ever wanted to be a cop. Maybe it was just because Rook had threatened the woman I loved, but I really wanted to catch bad guys right now.

"Yes, you do. I want Leo to name drop Marcus to Bishop and start a file with his name. No information in the file, just a blank file with his name. Marcus frequented that club Serena was working, so if anyone asks, you got his name that way. If Bishop or anyone else asks, you're just looking into the cops at that strip club to see if Serena turned any of them. Serena is going to be the big baddy right now. No mention of Rook to anyone. I'm working on things in the background and if you fuck this up for me, I'll fuck things up for all of you. Understand?" Ziva asked.

That woman certainly didn't take any shit. We all just grunted and nodded. She ordered Casey to call Leo and disconnected. It looked like it was going to be another day of doing nothing until Leo started that file and someone looked at it.

15

The FBI was supposed to be our ace in the hole. Our big weapon against Rook. I was starting to think they were playing this huge game with us. Ziva was lying. I already knew her tell. She'd start rapidly clicking her pen every time a lie came out her mouth. That pen started clicking every time she said all they were doing were watching until they had Rook and a plan. I had no idea if that meant they knew who Rook was, they just didn't have evidence to prove it or they didn't have anything more than we did.

Casey had already put her plan to work. Leo brought Marcus' name to Bishop and reported back Bishop was furious he had nothing except a hunch and a strip club. Andre and I were glued to Leo and Bishop's computers. Bishop was doing what he always did—he had Marcus' personnel file up and just looked like he stared at it for hours. No one had gotten into Leo's computer for days.

Milo hadn't checked in since the FBI had taken over aside from when he wanted to talk to Aiden about Granny. I had no idea if Milo was assisting or if he just thought Ziva and Eckart could handle this. He wasn't answering when I called either. Aiden said he wasn't talking about the investigation with him. He was just sharing memories about Granny. If Aiden asked, Milo just said investigations took time, but they would get the bastard like they always did.

We seemed to be doing nothing for days until Andre finally caught someone in Leo's computer again. They seemed to know exactly where they were going this time. Instead of opening all his new case files, they went straight to Marcus' file, opened it, saw there was nothing in it, and closed it within the span of ten minutes.

The ten minutes was still enough time for us to catch the IP. It was a VPN again and as soon as Andre told me someone was in Leo's computer, I ran my program and had their real IP. My program had already been uploaded, so I slid right into a conversation between a man and Serena on webcam. Casey peered over my shoulder and informed me it was Marcus.

I tried to look at the room Serena was in to see if I could pinpoint her location. It appeared to be a closet. I couldn't tell much because the door was closed. I couldn't even get anything about Rook because there only seemed to be women's clothing in the closet. I tried to just focus on the conversation.

"I don't see why you can't get me a safe house," Marcus complained. "They are going to find me eventually. I'm not stupid enough to run like Pete, but you know what's going to happen to me if I end up in jail like Dillion and Jake."

Serena had this look in her eyes like she was totally insane. She just sneered at Marcus. "You'd do well to remember what happened to Grant if someone wants information about things you don't need to be talking about. Take your beatings like a man. We'll get you out eventually and you'll have a house to hide in."

"I didn't sign up for this, Queen. I was promised I would never be caught as long as I followed orders. What if they get into my computer?"

I let out a maniacal laugh, wondering what I was going to find there. Andre started clacking keys.

"Let's make a copy of his hard drive while he's chatting," Andre chuckled.

Serena just rolled her eyes. "We overlook your little habits, but if you didn't insist on videotaping the entire thing, you wouldn't have to worry about your fucking hard drive. Maybe you should delete the entire spank bank. That shit Sullivan can't let this go and he's got hacker friends."

"Maybe you should have just run instead of planting that bomb."

"Please," Serena scoffed. "I only wish it would have taken out Sullivan in the blast. I'm going to make every single one of them regret disrupting our little game. Especially that damned girl. I've got no idea what's so special about her except her money that everyone, including Yakov, wants to fuck her so badly they keep fucking everything up. Rook and I have plans for her and Sullivan. When I get her, I'm going to fuck up that pretty face of hers."

Casey just growled, but this was what we needed. Serena live on cam blabbing her plans so we could keep Misty safe. Apparently, Casey too.

"I don't want to be a part of that," Marcus whined. "I know what you have on me, but I've done everything you and Rook asked. I've tampered with evidence, *stolen* evidence, and I've planted evidence to arrest the wrong man more than once. Please, just let me go to the safehouse."

Serena let out the same hyena laugh we all heard on the security footage when she was trashing Aiden's shop. I don't think it was a sound any of us would forget. It was like the last sound you heard in a haunted asylum before the crazed serial killer took your head off with a chainsaw.

"Marcus, right now, you're bait. Rook knows you caught Sullivan's eye because of *The Depraved Palace*. If you don't want your little habit getting you arrested, lay low and permanently silence anyone at the club that had the unfortunate luck of ending up on your hard drive. Tie up those loose ends and I'll talk to Rook about getting you to a safe house."

Serena disconnected and I looked over at Misty. She didn't look scared, she looked furious.

"If I ever meet that woman, I'm going to punch her in the throat so hard, she can't let out that awful laugh again. Were you able to get anything on her?"

"No, but Ziva is going to want to see what's on Marcus' hard drive. It looks like some of the dancers at *The Depraved Palace* are human trafficking victims. Marcus got them when they were underaged and when they got too old for him, they must have gone there.

That must be what Serena means by silencing the loose ends," Andre said grimly.

"I don't get it," Aiden said, scratching his beard. "If two of Rook's players were involved in that place, why was a sting arranged there?"

"There are *a lot* of cops that go to that club," Casey said. "I don't know if they were all Rook's or he was looking for a mass recruiting session."

"Maybe the club was becoming a liability," Misty said. "Maybe a decent cop got invited and suspected what was going on. He brought it to Bishop or someone else, Rook found out, and manipulated Serena into position to recruit as many people as possible on the way out. Or, maybe one of their girls escaped."

"We're going to have to tell Ziva about the club and Marcus' hard drive," Casey sighed. "I get the feeling she wasn't joking when she said she'd arrest all of us if we fucked this up."

I already knew she wasn't. I already knew Ziva was damned good at her job and if anyone could get Rook, it was going to be her. I just hated the fact that I knew she was lying to us about something. I knew she wasn't lying to us about the fact that Eckart would catch Andre and me if we tried to peek on their computers about the investigation. I already knew this from the computer I was sent.

Ziva looked like she was ready to pounce when Casey called. He told her about the conversation while Andre was emailing her what we found on the hard drive. Casey looked angry.

"Are you just going to sit back while Marcus

murders a bunch of girls at this club because you don't want to tip Rook off?"

"Let me call Patel. I wasn't originally sent down here to chase a New Orleans boogeyman. I was sent to partner with another rep about a strip club. I was supposed to be prepped when I got here, but she had a funeral to go to. I agreed as a personal favor to Milo to arrange that conference room and just listen. Milo was kind of my mentor for a while. After I called and said Milo's boogeyman was real, I was reassigned. Patel can tell us if Rook's club is the same club."

Ziva didn't feel the need to make that call over webcam where we'd all be in the loop. She picked up her cell phone and called, so we only got one side of the conversation and it was a lot of *uh huhs* and *yeahs* on our end before she hung up. When she hung up, I wondered if she was going to be in a sharing mood or that fucking pen was going to start clicking again. It was already in her left hand, where it always was.

"Rook arranged a bust on the club because a girl escaped. She didn't go to the police. She may have been held hostage by Marcus and that was why. She came to the FBI's attention and we've been working with Interpol. The reason Rook hasn't followed through with his bust is because we set her up like a Jane Doe overdose in Shreveport. Rook had to have seen it. Marcus isn't killing anyone at that club because Patel is raiding it any day now."

"If the FBI knows there's human trafficking there, why haven't you yet?"

Ziva sighed and her pen wasn't clicking. "The same reason we haven't raided the house Dillion and Jake are staying at yet. We don't want bouncers and bartenders. We want the men running the trafficking ring. The higher-ups. Getting them stops it, not arresting minor players. Patel will be joining our investigation since she has more information on the club owners. Maybe we can find Rook that way."

I already knew Ziva and Patel wouldn't find anything that tied to Rook at *The Defiant Palace*. There would be a knight running things and no paper trail to tie back to Rook.

16

When the mysterious Patel finally joined us the next day, she was a lot more forthcoming than Ziva about what was going on behind the scenes. Patel was a total hard ass. She wore her black hair pulled back in a severe bun and she looked like she took even less shit than Ziva did. She gave us a lot of information, but she didn't have a tell like Ziva did. She spent the entire call downing black coffee and chain smoking.

"Has this Marcus deleted evidence off his hard drive yet? What you downloaded can't be used because of the way you obtained it," Patel said.

"No, for some reason, it's still there, despite Serena's warning."

Patel snorted. "I watched the videos. He considers it art, that's why he hasn't deleted it. I suspect he thinks he will kill a few girls, Rook will get him to a safe house, and he can bring his filthy rape videos with him."

"How exactly is this going to play out without

spooking Rook? That's why we're waiting, right?" Aiden asked.

"Easy," Patel snapped, lighting another cigarette. "Two separate raids. One on the club, one on the filthy rapist's house. When we talk about it, we'll say we got a sketch of Marcus from our Jane Doe and pretend like since we have Marcus, the case is closed. I'm guessing Rook and Serena don't ask to see his personal collection of videos or that horrid mask he wears while he's taping himself. Rook will think the girl that escaped ruined this side business and was able to identify Marcus. He already knows about the man's proclivities and seems to be okay with them. We can raid the club without ruining Ziva's investigation."

"Can you arrange the raid before Marcus hurts any of those women? What if he's got a girl at his house right now that needs saving?" Misty asked.

"It's almost a certainty Marcus has some poor girl chained up at his house. I'm not dallying with this. Even with this new information about Rook, I'm not changing my plans. The raid on the club happens tonight. Since you brought me a new name, I just had to add a secondary raid on that shit stain's house."

"Are you working with local law enforcement?" Casey asked.

"I was going to. I need more law enforcement. Given the current swamp you have here, I can't trust anyone. You can't be there either, Casey," Patel said, her stern face finally softening. "If you somehow end up at an FBI raid when Serena and Rook already know you're finding his men, it'll tip them off. That goes for all of you. None of you can be anywhere near that club when this goes down."

"We mean it, Gareth," Ziva snapped. "Milo told us about all of you. If you plan to be just hanging out on the street minding your own business, I'll arrest your happy ass and keep you in a cell until all this Rook business is over."

Damn. Milo must have done profiles on all of us because that was exactly what I was going to do. I was going to see if there was a place on the street or a coffee shop or something I could just hang out at and watch the entire thing go down. Ziva and Patel didn't strike me as women who would miss a single thing. They also didn't strike me as women who made empty threats. They'd both lock my happy ass up if I even breathed in too close a vicinity to *The Defiant Palace* while the raid was going on.

Patel finally smiled. She had a nice, friendly smile and I wasn't even sure she was capable of cracking one. "I'm going to give you boys a little present. They just passed a new law requiring us to wear body cams for raids. With the laptops went sent you, you can watch the entire thing like pay per view. Keep in mind, I'm only telling you this because you gave me Marcus and I don't want any of you there fucking this up for me and Ziva. Eight tonight. Run a program called *Big Brother* and you'll see all the active cams. Narrow the search field to New Orleans and you'll find the only two going down that night. Happy and are you keeping your asses far away from my raids?"

I was about to pinky swear, but Andre spoke first. "You're bringing down a human trafficking ring, a rapist, and one of Rook's money makers. Casey and Gareth will be *here,* watching and celebrating with us. I'm going to make a five-course meal and an elaborate dessert to celebrate. We haven't had many victories with Rook and we need to celebrate the small ones."

"Another Doberge cake?" Misty said hopefully. I wasn't surprised she asked. Anyone who had Granny's Doberge cake would soon find it their favorite cake.

"Anything for you. I hope all of you are prepared because I'm breaking out the big guns for our celebration meal."

"Thank you, Andre," Ziva sighed with relief. "Milo told me you were an excellent cook. Maybe when all of this is over, I'll actually be able to taste your version of celebration food."

"I would be happy to cook for all of you that bring down Rook. You all have a standing reservation for dinner here when this is over."

"Tonight is just the start," Ziva said. "Let's see how Marcus likes being questioned by two women who can fight back."

I knew I wasn't the only one who hoped Ziva and Patel knocked him around a bit for what he did to all those women.

17

We were all antsy and rowdy except for Andre, who banned everyone, including Misty, from the kitchen while he made his feast. Aiden had finished coming out of his funk. Misty's cake and his birthday started it and this bust had him laughing again. Casey and I were on edge and pacing, wanting to see heads getting cracked. Aiden was just so happy *someone* was finally getting arrested, he had his music on and was dancing with Misty.

We could all dance. Granny was insistent us kids were going to grow into men with manners. I may have gone the total opposite of that until I met Misty, but Granny taught us all proper dances none of us thought we would ever need. Not even the girls at our school dances knew the dances Granny taught us. Our Misty had years of dance training. I had no idea if she knew Granny spent hours teaching us these dances, but Aiden's eyes were a little glazed over as Misty as able to do every single one with him while we waited.

I was glued to my laptop watching Marcus' laptop. If he tried to delete those files, I was pretty sure he wouldn't think to empty the trash. I'd just restore the files so they were there when the FBI barged in. Marcus didn't come to his laptop the entire time I was watching. I didn't want to think about what he was doing away from his laptop based on the videos there. What kept my mind off it was that soon, whoever was locked in his house would be free and Marcus could give us Rook.

By the time the raid rolled around, Aiden was drunk and singing and I was just shaking my head. Marcus had no idea what was going to hit him. Andre finally came out and told us we were eating in the formal dining room. While we were eating, he'd brought a plasma TV in there and had hooked up his laptop.

"For the first course, we have Fried Green Tomato Caprese, followed by chilled watermelon and jalapeno soup. I've got a shrimp salad next, then my mother's secret gumbo recipe. For dessert, Granny's Doberge cake for Misty and Aiden," Andre said proudly.

My mouth was practically watering. Reena's gumbo recipe *and* Granny's Doberge cake? I'd just about died and gone to heaven. Andre started bringing out trays and fired up the video. He made it split screen. I saw a house and the outside of *The Defiant Palace*. They seemed to be just watching. Andre handed me the remote so we could switch between the sound on the cameras.

When the word was finally given, I watched men and women storm Marcus' house and the club. Marcus tried to run and so did several people from the club.

Marcus was tackled and handcuffed. I focused on Marcus' house first because I was worried about the girl inside. I think we were all holding our breath when Ziva started kicking doors in and finally found a drugged girl handcuffed to a steel bed.

Ziva held the girl while she sobbed, then led her out to an ambulance that was waiting. We watched her talk to a man who had already bagged Marcus' laptop. They were sweeping the entire house, but they'd already arrested Marcus and found his prisoner, so I switched back to the club.

The club was pandemonium. People running and screaming everywhere. It had my blood pumping. They were chasing bouncers and patrons all over the place. Patel didn't seem to be worried about that. She was moving towards the back of the club. I saw several dirty rooms that girls appeared to be kept prisoner in. I was shocked Patel also took the time to comfort them while they cried before she moved to the next room.

We watched the club for hours before it was empty of people. We'd mowed through Andre's entire meal and now we were just drinking. Andre made Sazeracs for all of us and we were all getting drunk. I watched through Patel's camera as the last van drove off.

"If you run the program *1984* tomorrow, you can watch us interrogate Marcus and the owner of the club," she whispered into her mic before she turned it off.

We were going to have to stop drinking because I think we all wanted to watch that. Maybe we would get Rook. Aiden was drunker than all of us and wanted to continue celebrating. I hoped we would all crash on the sectional again, but Misty pulled him off to his bedroom so he wouldn't disturb us. I wandered off to my bedroom so I could get some shut eye too.

Maybe tomorrow, we'd have Rook.

18

We were all pretty hung over the next morning, but Aiden was especially feeling bad. Andre was the least hung over. Probably not at all. He had hangover food prepared and the sectional already arranged when we finally all stumbled out.

"Eat quickly. Patel is questioning Marcus in thirty minutes," Andre said.

Eating quickly while you had a hangover was just asking to barf everywhere, but we all did it anyway. My stomach was lurching when we finally spilled into the living room. Andre had arranged the sectional like a huge couch bed. We all spread out and Misty draped herself across us. Her back was over my lap, so I started giving her a massage.

The TV was already hooked to Andre's FBI laptop and turned on. We were looking at an empty interrogation room, but it wasn't empty for long. Patel and Marcus finally came in. Marcus looked like shit. It looked like he had been weeping all night. Patel's full mouth widened into a cruel grin.

"That's a hell of a shiner," she taunted.

Marcus just burst into tears again. "I swear, I'll do whatever you want if you put me in a good prison. A prison I can be protected in."

"A prison you won't be raped in, you mean. A prison Rook can get you out of, perhaps?"

"How do you—Rook, he—Oh, God, I'm in such deep shit," he stammered, burying his face in his hands.

"Care to tell me how deep this shit goes? Who is Rook?"

"I swear to you, I don't know. When I was in college, I was being investigated for serial rape among the sorority houses. The cop who was up my ass promised me an out if I kept my nose clean and did what was asked of me. He even promised me women I could keep for a while so I wouldn't get caught. I was so careful. How did you find out?"

"The cop who approached you. What was his name? How does Rook and Serena play into this?"

"I went to college out of state. I'm not from here. The cop, his name was Higgins and this was in California. I was told Higgins would make the charge go away and I was now becoming a cop instead of an engineer. I joined the force in California, but almost as soon as I got my badge, Higgins told me to put in a transfer to New Orleans. I didn't meet Serena until she joined the force much later. She's insane!"

"And Rook?"

"Higgins told me I would be working for him before I moved to New Orleans and Serena seems to know him. I've never met the man, nor do I know who he is. Serena likes to taunt me with him. She says he's responsible for the women I get and if I don't do something he asks, they'll both expose me. If I mention either of them when I'm taken into custody, I'll die in my cell. You have to help me! I'm telling you what I know. You have to keep me safe!"

"You haven't given me much, Marcus. Where is Serena hiding? Can you at least give me that?"

Marcus looked like he was about to get hysterical. "There's safehouses. Jake and Dillion, do you know about them too? They are still here. I don't have the addresses. I don't know where the safehouses are or where they are all staying, but Jake, Serena, and Dillion are still in New Orleans!"

Patel looked like she was wanting to fidget without her cigarettes, but was managing to keep herself still. Her face never betrayed anything. I was waiting for her to tell Marcus he wasn't giving her anything she didn't already know. She just stood calmly.

"That's all the questions I have, Marcus," she said, standing to leave.

"Wait!" Marcus yelled. "I want your word you'll keep me safe. I told you things my life has been threatened over. I know I can't avoid jail, but I want a nice, *safe* prison."

"You aren't in any position to make demands, you disgusting little worm," Patel snapped. "Bring him back to his cell," she said sticking her head out the door. A huge agent came in and I was happy to see him manhandle Marcus as he yanked him out the room.

We had no idea what Patel was doing and if she was

done until she called Casey. The conversation was brief and all she gave him was a room number. Andre got up to fix the computer and the screen changed to a room with a man none of us knew. He was this small, squirrely looking man who had *Killer* misspelled on his forehead. It looked like a prison tattoo or something that was done by a drunk four-year-old someone gave a tattoo gun to. The rest of his tattoos weren't any better. God, I was starting to sound like Aiden, giving critiques on people's tattoos.

This dude was nothing like Marcus. He had his arms crossed and was scowling at Patel. She just sat and stared, I guess waiting for him to break. He must have been dumber than shit to say what he said to Patel.

"If I had known you were coming, I would have had a Devil's Breath cocktail waiting for you and prepared a room. You look like you've got a hot little body under that power suit. I could have made a lot of money pimping your ass out to men who like brown women."

We all growled at this racist little pimp, but Patel didn't even blink. "You certainly could have tried, but we still would have ended up right here, Francis."

"My name is Pyro," he growled.

"Your name is Francis Darcy. You spent time in prison for public masturbation in the middle of a romantic comedy that's currently sitting at four percent on Rotten Tomatoes. The sappiness overwhelmed you and you just *had* to whip it out?"

I snorted and Misty started giggling. We really shouldn't be. This Francis went on to do some really awful shit, but it was nice to watch Patel utterly humiliate him.

"If I wasn't handcuffed to this table, you wouldn't *dare* say shit like that to me. You have no idea the shit you've gotten yourself into poking your nose into this club. I'm not going to serve any time for this."

"Rook isn't going to get you out of this, Francis. Did you think we didn't know about him? Perhaps you missed it when we were storming your club since you were in the back beating a girl, but I'm FBI, not local PD."

We were all watching Francis' reaction to that. It was going to tell us if Rook's reach extended to the federal level too. I rested my elbows on Misty's back and intently studied the plasma screen. Rook made a lot of people a lot of promises about not getting caught and had apparently given women for service, but did he promise anything on the federal level?

Francis gulped and shifted in his chair. That could mean anything. His thin, rubbery lips were in a grim line. "Rook always protects his people," Francis said stubbornly.

"We raided your apartment above the club and we know how he was paying you. You won't be getting meth in here and we're tracing the money transfers. You cashed your cut and stashed it in your mattress, but Rook's money was wire transferred to a shell corporation. Rook won't be able to protect you when we find him. You'd do better to tell us what you know about Rook."

"I ain't a squealer, lady. And I got no reason to trust you. Rook's taken care of me for a long time. Even if he don't have someone on the inside in here, he'll get one. You don't know him like I do. He'll get me out for staying loyal and he'll kill me for squealing. And I ain't got a name for you anyway."

"Maybe you'll decide to be a little more forthcoming when you start detoxing off all the drugs we found in your apartment. Your blood is probably pure meth and cocaine."

"I ain't no rat, lady, not even if you make me dry out. I ain't even probably got the information you want anyway."

"Try me."

Man, Francis walked right into that one. He shifted again and I was starting to wonder if he'd already started detoxing. He was very thin and not an attractive man. He had this look kind of like a weasel for someone who kept saying he wasn't a rat. He was writhing more and more in his chair and his pale face looked like a sheen of sweat was starting to break out in the harsh lighting in the room. Patel still looked calm and under control, but it looked like Francis was slipping.

"I got nothing, okay? I ain't got a name or face. I got a routing number and an account number to send money to. I send money, I get my share, I get drugs, and I can fuck any of the girls I want. Fuck, I don't even know where the girls come from. There's this dude that just drops them off after he's broken them in, but fuck if I know where they came from."

"What about a woman who calls herself Queen?"

"No way. I ain't saying a single word about that woman. She's fucking crazy. She'd walk straight through the front door of this building and kill anyone in her way just to gut me for talking. Or she'd blow up the whole fucking building just because I was inside."

"When was the last time she was at your club?"

"It could have been fucking ten years ago and it would have been too soon for me. Even the bouncers were scared of her. It was like she practically moved in and was fucking things up for about two months, then she just ass up disappeared. I didn't ask where she went because I didn't want her to come back."

"She has no idea where you are and she'd be arrested on sight if she showed her face anywhere near this building."

"You could *try* to arrest her. She'd kill anyone who tried. Bitch is crazy."

"That's all I have for you, Francis. Unless you find yourself with more information you're hiding from me, you're going to be looking at four walls for a very long time."

We took down Rook's club and Patel and Ziva had two of his men in custody. But we still had no idea who Rook was. Another dead end. A call came in on Andre's computer and it was Ziva. I wondered if she was in a sharing mood or she'd be clicking her pen again.

"Just to update all of you, we've already frozen the bank accounts associated with the club. Patel sent her partner in this to talk to your Bishop. Bishop will be doing the press conference, but he's being told the story we came down on the club because of a girl that escaped that we helped. This way, everyone at the station will hear the FBI took down *The Defiant Palace* over an escapee, we've wrapped up our investigation, and we are leaving. The real investigation is still ongoing, but no one at the station will know the truth."

"Did you find out anything about the shell corporation? I can look into it," I said, wanting something to do.

"No, Gareth. Milo told me what you did when you found the other one. We've located the accounts and frozen them. We've also located any real estate associated with it and we have people watching. That club was a multi-million-dollar cash cow for Rook. The loss of that money is going to make him careless, which is what we want. We stationed surveillance outside of all the property before we did anything. Rook will know we know the location of some of his safehouses and if there's anyone living there, he'll want to move them. If his Queen is staying in one, he'll get her out. We may be able to get Serena with this, which may draw Rook out in the open."

"No," Aiden said, shaking his head. "Rook is staying at a house that doesn't have any association with his shell corporations. Serena is his lover. They fucked in my shop after they trashed it. Rook wants Serena close to him. She won't be in a safe house, she'll be staying with Rook in a house that has no ties to his dealings."

Ziva raised an eyebrow at Aiden. "You're a tattoo artist, right? You think like one of us. All of you do. That's the *only* reason I'm not demanding to only speak to Casey. I need all five of you to figure this out."

She wasn't clicking her pen and I was so glad she said that to Aiden. I knew he had been hung up about being the only one of us without a skill to bring Rook down. He'd had some damned good ideas and we tried to tell him that, but I think hearing it directly from Ziva finally got it to sink in for him.

Ziva's pen started clicking. I knew whatever she was

about to tell us was going to be a half-truth again. "We need to see if our ruse has paid off. Casey sent me all of Rook's text messages. He sends one when you've disturbed his game or he's made a major move to hurt one of you. Your homework today is to just relax and wait to see if Rook texts that he's onto us. He'll be planning something big and he seems to like bragging to Casey. We want Rook careless and if he texts, that will give us a hint."

Ziva disconnected and her homework was a good idea. I just wanted to know what she *wasn't* telling us. I wanted to get my personal laptop and go poking around in things to find out what Ziva was hiding from us, but I knew damned well they'd catch me and I didn't have enough information to look anywhere else except the FBI computers.

We just sat and waited. The text never came. We made a major move on the chess board and Rook didn't know what was coming. I had no idea what the FBI had planned. I knew Ziva was hiding something from us. I knew I wouldn't find out what until she chose to tell us either.

We still didn't have a name or face for Rook and I knew we wouldn't until he got careless. But this was a victory today that needed to be celebrated. Andre *never* let us do this. It was like it was against his religion to have food delivered.

"We need to celebrate and I want to show Misty a little more of New Orleans," I said, clapping my hands. "We can't take her there yet, but we can order Tavolinos. Misty would love the *Fungi Bianco* pizza and we also need to get a Buffalo Chicken and Spinach Artichoke pizza."

"Gourmet pizza?" Misty said, perking up.

Andre loved going to eat at Tavolinos, but if he was home, he cooked instead of having it ordered. I had no idea if he was going to insist tonight, but he saw that sparkle in Misty's eyes that none of us can resist. Andre got excited too.

"Misty needs to try the Wild Boar and Polpette," Andre said, nodding.

"What do they have for dessert? We need dessert for this celebration," Misty laughed.

"I love a girl that eats," Andre growled, pulling her into his lap. "They have Tiramisu, Black and White Mousse, and a cake called Chocolate Madness."

Misty gave Andre a deep kiss. She had no idea this was the first time we'd ever had food delivered here. "Just get all three and we can all share."

Andre went to place the order. This was a celebration and I already knew how it was going to end. I was just remembering Aiden's birthday. The Chocolate Madness was my favorite.

I was hoping part of the celebration was that Misty ended up in my lap with us feeding each other Chocolate Madness. Things were definitely starting to look up for us.